FEARING THE UNKNOWN

Published by Spines
ISBN: 979-8-89383-504-5

FEARING THE UNKNOWN

KAREN ROTELLA LEWIS

DEDICATION

I would like to Dedicate my book to the man in my life for supporting me while writing and thank My friend Mark McNary for the Encouragement To my children Jeanmarie, Anthony, and Angela, and also to my best friend Maureen Wilk for always being there for me and helping me through my struggles.

CONTENTS

ABOUT THE AUTHOR

Karen Rotella Lewis. Rotella is my maiden name. I have 3 great children two beautiful Girls, Angela Christian Bocchino Solcberg and Jean Marie Lewis, and a handsome son, Anthony Bocchino fourth. I have two handsome grandsons, Isacc Acevedo MR, and Thomas Meade. These children of mine and grandchildren deserve a happy good life. I wish them success in everything they do. PLEASE PLEASE LOOK AFTER EACH OTHER AND KEEP EACH OTHER SAFE.

I grew up in Poughkeepsie NY. On the 27th of October 1964, my mom and dad got divorced. My hobbies are beading, making jewelry, writing, and gaming. I love to play Elden Ring Never Winter and Elder scrolls. I like Virtual reality, I am a horror movie fan and have a great passion for horror stories. I am a writer by profession, I have an electric guitar and I'm also learning to play thc Alto saxophone and currently learning violin as well. I love spending time with my children and grandchildren.

CHAPTER 1

IT'S TIME FOR SPRING BREAK

"Two beers, please!" Jason ordered the bartender as he approached the bar counter.

"Sure, sir!" The bartender said and turned to get Jason's drinks. While Jason waited by the counter, he saw Lily dancing near the jukebox.

"Hey Lily, you had your drink?" Jason shouted as he saw Lily dancing. So, he thought about asking Lily about the drink as well. But she was too lost in the music. The music was loud so she didn't catch a word of what Jason said. Jason took his drink and came back to the booth they were all sitting in.

It was Saturday evening, Jason and Lily along with Mike, Mary, and Ted had come to a *"Wink Wink Bar"* to enjoy the evening. All five of them were high school friends with different interests in life united together by a single motive, to enjoy themselves.

Lily and Mary were enjoying the beats and the music while the boys were having drinks on the rocks. All five of them were high school friends and were fond of traveling and partying around.

"Where are the girls?" Ted asked as he kept his phone down.

Lily and Mary were best friends with opposite personalities but golden hearts. Mary was a bit timid with hazel brown hair, blue eyes, braced teeth, and a kind helping nature. One thing about Mary that made her an exception in the group was her love for books and literature. She would love to spend most of her time diving into her books. She wasn't as bold as Lily, but still, they were close.

On the other hand, Lily was a modern girl who loved music and loved to dance. She always stood by Mary's side. Lily was least interested in her studies.

"Oh, are you done scorching the social media?" Mike said sarcastically and he gave Jason a high-five here, "They're rocking the floor," Mike replied pointing toward the girls. Ted turned around to look at the girls. He saw Lily dancing her feet out. However, Mary was just slightly moving her body.

All five of them were *The Famous Five* at their school. Though they owned entirely different personalities, still they were tied up as friends.

After getting tired of dancing, Lily and Mary came towards the table where Jason, Mike, and Ted were seated. Lily was panting, she took the beer from Jason's hand and took a sip.

"Having a beer without me?" Lily complained weirdly staring at Jason.

"I asked you if you had anything to drink but you were too busy dancing," replied Jason.

"Well, you should've gotten me a drink anyways," said Lily while smiling and winking at Jason.

Jason smiled smugly and said, "Right! Why don't you just leave Mike here and go out with me instead? Then I'll be sure to get your drinks and everything you need proactively."

"Hey! Shut up man!" Mike indulged.

"I'm just kidding dude!" Jason said to Mike while Lily broke into laughter.

They all were chatting about random things when Mike asked them about their plans for spring break. One by one they started sharing their ideas about the spring breaks. Mike, Ted, Lily, and even Mary loved camping and going on an adventure.

"Well, I'm off to Florida to enjoy myself. There's a party at my friend's place," Jason told his friends about his plans.

However, none of his friends were surprised by Jason's plan. Everyone knew that Jason was a party animal. He loved chilling around and partying hard. So, he wasn't part of the camping plan Ted and Mike had.

"Hey, guys, how about we go camping in the woods!" Mary exclaimed as she loved exploring the woods, hiking, and going out for an adventure.

"Great idea, it would be perfect for our camping though," Ted agreed excitedly.

Ted, Mike, Lily, and Mary loved camping in the woods. All of them were always in search to discover something new and thrilling. Last summer, they went camping in the woods of Alabama. They always ensured that the camping location they selected was loaded with excitement and thrilling adventure.

"There are some woods over an hour away from the place where I lived previously!" Mary told them to create suspense.

"And what is so special about them!" Ted questioned

her wondering why she suggested those particular woods.

Mary had just recently moved her home, the location where her previous home had creepy woods around. There were many myths around about forests and many people who went into the forest never returned home. Many people said that the place was haunted and that it was a breeding ground for demons. It was the reason why Mary had moved. However, this bunch didn't believe in all these things.

"Hey, guys you know what?" Lily said attracting her attention toward herself.

"Do you know these woods around Mary's home are also known as *the disappearing woods?*" Lily told her friends as they were staring at her wide, almost believing her story.

"Why?" Ted and Mike asked in chorus. Jason ignored every word Lily was saying. Jason was scared of creepy places and was scared of the names of the devil and demon. So, to hide his fear, he just rolled his eyes.

"My grandma told me when dad was five and he was returning from his school. He would walk home with Jake every day," Lily told her friends.

"And who was Jake?" Mike asked developing his interest in what Lily was saying.

"He was my dad's friend, duh!" Lily replied making a bizarre face as Mike interrupted her conversation.

"Shhhhh, Mike. Let her speak man," Ted said hitting Mike on his head.

"Okay, coming back to the incident! One day when dad and Jake were on their way back home, suddenly dad's friend screamed. As dad turned around Jake was nowhere to be found," Lily finished the story.

There was silence for a few minutes, then they all burst out into laughter. They couldn't help themselves. Mike and Ted started making fun of the myths of the jungle.

"Ooooh, I'm scared! The demons are gonna take me!" Mike said acting to be terrified. Ted couldn't help his laughter and burst out. Mike's expression made him laugh like hell.

"Stop it, you guys! Even I've heard that last year a whole crew disappeared while camping in the same woods." Mary said trying to console Lily. Mary knew how easily Lily would get offended when anyone made her a laughing stock in public.

"Very funny," Lily answered as she was a bit agitated. Lily didn't like to be made fun of, she always wanted to look smart and intelligent among her friends.

"Okay, friends, jokes apart. Are we on for the

disappearing woods?" Ted asked, he was still giggling slightly.

"I'm in!" Lily said raising up her hand.

"Me too!" Mary and Mike answered in chorus.

"Jason? What about you?" Lily asked Jason. Though she knew Jason had other plans she wanted to ensure that he didn't end up missing the fun.

"I've got better plans waiting," Jason answered sounding least interested in their program.

"Okay, guys then we will set off on coming Saturday," Mike said looking at everyone. Each one seemed to agree with him. They were now all set with their spring break programs at their back. Mike, Ted, Lily, and Mary started to plan the camping trip and discussed everything that was needed.

Whenever the friends had anywhere to go, Mike would readily pick them up. He belonged to a well-off family, his dad owned a business and he could have literally anything he wanted. However, he wasn't a rich spoiled brat. The friends finalized their plan and Jason was looking at them trying to wonder if the myths of the disappearing forest were true, then there was no chance his friends would return alive. A chill ran down his spine, but he still didn't count himself in for the camping.

"Hungry anyone?" Lily asked her friends as in the excitement of deciding on the camping trip they almost skipped their dinner.

"Me, I'm starving," Mary answered as she couldn't stay hungry for very long.

Once the friends were all set for their camping plan, they decided to leave the bar and get something to eat.

All got up and headed towards Mike's jeep. His dad gave him a jeep on his last birthday. One by one they hopped in the jeep and off they went. It was 3:00 am and there were hardly any restaurants open. After driving for 30 minutes, they saw a restaurant, Mike quickly turned the jeep towards the restaurant. Each one of them got off the jeep.

"I'll go park the car!" Mike said as he drove to the parking. The restaurant they had chosen was right in front of a dark creepy forest. After parking his jeep, Mike got out of the jeep. He suddenly saw a shadowy figure in the woods. At first, he thought it was his imagination and started walking toward the restaurant where his friends awaited him.

Once he got inside, they all ordered the food and waited for the food to be served. While the food was being served, Mike tried to convince Jason to join them on the camping trip. He wanted all five of them on the trip.

"Jason, are you sure about this?" Mike asked Jason about joining them on the trip.

"About what?" Jason questioned giving Mike a stinky look.

"Coming with us on the camping trip, into the disappearing woods?" Mike replied.

"It's a clear NO!" Jason answered with fear in his eyes. He couldn't forget what Lily had told them about the woods. He was better off with his Florida party plans.

Everyone tried to convince him but he didn't agree. So, they still gave him the time to rethink. At last, Mike told him with a crooked smile, "You wouldn't want to miss the fun, Jason!"

They were just discussing the adventure when their order arrived. Being too hungry, they all begin to eat. Once they were done with the food, Mike and Lily ordered ice creams for themselves. After having the dinner, Ted cleared the bill while the others headed towards the jeep. Mike went to bring the jeep, but he was surprised when he saw his jeep. The left rear-proof mirror of the jeep was cracked. He was shocked wondering who could have done this.

"What's taking you so long?" Ted asked him as he walked towards his jeep to see what the matter was.

"Who did this?" Ted asked as he too was shocked.

"I dunno!" Mike said and got into the jeep. He drove the jeep to the place where his friends were awaiting him. They all jumped in the jeep and Mike dropped each of them at their homes.

While Mike was on his way back home, he wondered who broke the mirror of his jeep. He then began to overthink everything.

Who was the shadowy figure, I saw in the woods? That was a remote area! Mike was deep in his thoughts when suddenly a dog came in front of the jeep. Luckily his foot was on the brake and he was successful in stopping the jeep. When he got off the jeep to see if anything had happened to the dog. He was surprised to see that there was no sign of a dog on the entire street.

Mike wasn't surprised anymore, he was shocked. He quickly got into his jeep and fled as fast as he could. His heart was pounding loudly, he wasn't in his senses. It was the third incident that he had faced that night. He couldn't understand what was going on. He drove as fast as he could and stopped when he reached his home.

Mike was terrified. After parking his jeep, he went straight to his room. The same was stuck in his mind, but he thought maybe he was just assuming things and there was nothing around. So, ignoring it all he took a shower and went straight to bed.

Trrrrrrrrrr…. Trrrrrrrrrrrrr…! Mike woke up with a heavy head, he looked around and realized it was his alarm. He immediately got up to set off for school. It was a big day for him and his friends.

Mike and Ted were some of the best basketball players in their college and they had their inter-colleges match. Mike, after getting ready got in his jeep and went straight to the college.

Jason and Ted were waiting for Mike near the college gate. Ted wanted to tell Mike about the match cancellation. As soon as they saw Mike, Ted ran towards him.

"All set for the match?" Mike asked as they punched their fists.

"Um… The match has been canceled," Ted replied.

"What? Why?" Mike asked him as he was unable to figure out the actual reason behind the sudden cancelation of the match.

The boys were just talking when Lily and Mary came there.

"We girls are going shopping, wanna join?" Lily asked Mike. She then saw Mike and Ted talking to each other. Both seemed a bit worried. As Mike and Ted came closer, they told their friends about the sudden cancelation of the basketball match. The reason was quite strange, the coach of the opposite team had suddenly disappeared into thin air. It was strange and creepy but their friends cheered them up and told them about the shopping plan.

Lily then nagged Mike and Ted asking whether they had talked to Jason about joining them on the camping trip.

"Did you ask him again?" Lily whispered to Ted and Mike as they walked towards the class.

"He is constantly refusing to join us and he has already started his packing for Florida!" Ted exclaimed.

"Last night, I called him, I told him I'm not taking no for an answer. But he said that all I have for you is a simple no," Ted continued.

CHAPTER 2

THE NIGHT OF TERRORS

A few weeks back…

The full moon is all that illuminates the black sky. John Denver's 'Take me Home' echoes through the dark forest as a group of college friends enjoy their time in the woods.

"Hey, Tim, why don't you tell them about what happened with your dad in the Vegas apartment," Sara exclaimed. Her sharp features made her expressions more evident. She wasn't up for any kind of excuses.

Tim clears his throat, puts his guitar aside, and begins to speak, "Ok, so, there was a time when mom and dad lived in Vegas. They were there for two years. And well, on most days they led their lives normally."

He leans forward to add a log to the campfire, and rubbing dust off his hands, he adds, "they did have some abnormal experiences, but there isn't much they have shared with me, besides this one story."

He takes another pause to scratch his nose, and continues, "Once, they were in their room, and heard the sound of the chairs moving. You know the sound of chairs screeching against wood when dragged. Yeah so, they heard the sound, and it was before me and Ted were born so naturally, they kind of freaked out."

"Oh, I bet," Sara agrees, running her fingers through Tim's long hair.

"So, dad went out of his room to see where the noise was coming from wondering if someone had broken into the house." He looked everywhere but couldn't find anything out of order."

Craig comments, "Maybe they were delusional about the whole ordeal."

"Hey, hey…" Tim takes a pause and widens his eyes to say, "Not done yet!..... So, he's looking around to find something out of place, and he notices the chairs are pulled out of the dining table. He tucks the chairs back inside and returns to his room. The next morning when he leaves the room, he finds the chairs pulled out again."

"Well, maybe your mom had pulled them out," Kate suspects.

"I had the same thing in mind, and so I asked. It turned out mom had slept late that night and wasn't even up when dad left the room." Tim clarifies.

"Did you guys have Casper at that time?" Sara curiously asks.

"No, Mom and Dad had no pets, so you can rule that out," Tim responds.

"So what are you saying?" Kate argues. Kate was rebellious just like her mother. She never believed in what she heard, in fact, she always disagreed with anything that did not make sense to her, even if it was coming from her teachers.

Having known her for long enough, Tim smirks, "I am not saying anything."

"No, you're saying your parents lived with ghosts in Vegas." Kate counters.

Tim has now lost his smile, "If they did not move the chairs, who did!"

Kate still wants to argue, but Nick, her boyfriend, gives her his soft looks, which are more of a request. It is something he does with his eyes and lips when he wants Kate to stop. Kate, usually, does not pay heed, but this time around she looks away without arguing any further. Nick takes off his red cap and puts it on

Kate pulling it all the way down and covering her eyes. She resists and fixes it in position.

"My turn… my turn….I have a story," Aron interrupts taking a puff and passing the joint to his girlfriend Charlotte.

The night is cold, and the group of seven are keeping themselves close to the campfire.

Aron continues, "Conant Park, New Jersey." He takes a pause glancing over each of them, "bet, none of you have heard!"

Before Aron can get along with his story, Tim speaks, "I hope it's not ghosts kidnapping girls in a van."

Aron grins with disappointment and responds, "Smarty pants….umnmn… ever been to the Union Hotel."

"No, is this another one of your Jersey stories," Tim responds with a smirk.

"Aron always likes hotels…isn't it? Must have been with Betty there." Charlotte fires a pun.

The rest giggle as Aron shrugs his shoulders raising his brows. "The story, guys, let's stick to that."

He receives a unified response as the remaining six fix his eyes on him to listen to the story.

Aron tightens his grip around Charlotte's waist who is sitting between his legs. He starts, "I was there with my father for two nights, which was right before we moved here."

He now has the attention of the gang.

"The first night as I was laying on the bed, suddenly, I heard voices of kids fighting with each other. I couldn't hear what they were saying, but something was not right. We were in the suite, so I immediately pushed myself out of bed and rushed to my father's room. Since he was sleeping, I didn't wake him up, but no way was I going to return to the room."

"Beers anybody…this is going to be a long story," Craig inquires with a giggle.

Aron passes him a stare. Tim and Kate ask for bottles. As bottles are being passed, he continues, "So I don't wanna go to my room, and I can't stay in his. My dad would call me a sisy if I did, that's how he is."

"I mean, he has a point," Craig attempts to put on a poker face, but fails to hold his smile.

The crew burst into laughter, the echoes of which can be heard from a distance. The night is getting deep, and the camp smoke is all that is moving in the wild forest, at least, from what the seven of them can see.

"I spend the night in his room and leave for mine in the early hours of the morning - hoping he does not find out. The next night I decided to try sleeping in my bed, but, of course, not for a moment could I find a second's sleep."

"Didn't you tell your dad about it?" Charlotte asks innocently.

"No, I mean, he wouldn't have believed me." He pauses to pull out a cigarette from the pack lying next to him. He lights it up and picks up the story from where he had paused, "the next night I begin to hear similar voices, and the voices are much louder now. I slowly pull out from the blanket.

I know something's not right, and as I get out of bed to leave my room, I see a woman standing in the hallway. I push her away and run to dad's room, but to my surprise, he's not there. I began sobbing wondering where he was.

I turn around to find her standing right behind me. Before I can make a move, she attempts to slice me with the dagger."

Silence prevails for the next five seconds, after which Tim decides to break it. "You're making this up aren't you."

"No, I am not," Aron is quick to respond.

"What happens next?" Tim questions.

"Well, suddenly, my eyes open wide as if popping out of my head. My body is split in half and my…"

"Shut up…this is absurd." Charlotte intervenes in the story.

Aron and Craig break up in laughter, and the rest call him out.

"Such a prick," Kate comments in anger.

Charlotte slaps his arm with her palm. Aron kisses her ear with her tongue as she pulls away. He then stands on his feet and begins heading toward the wood. "I need to pe-pe ya'll. Craig, save some of that pot for me."

He begins humming the song playing on the speaker system while walking away from the campsite.

"The night's still young, never gonna get old

Livin' for today like there's no tomorrow

Follow the grooves, the tires in the grass

Stayin' on the gas like we're never comin' back"

He turns back to see that he has walked some distance, as he can barely listen to the lyrics of the song. He picks a spot and begins to piss. He has a habit of whistling while pissing, especially when relieving himself in Mother Nature. Suddenly he feels something has moved past him. He looks in all directions, but cannot find anything. He stops whistling, wondering if it is what is attracting some wild creatures toward him.

The sound persists, but he refuses to lose his calm, "Oh man, Craig's got some good stash."

He feels something is there behind him as if there's movement behind the bushes. His Swiss knife lay in his bag in the camp. He knows he should have brought it, but there's nothing he can do about it now.

"Tim, try scaring Sara instead. You'll be better off playing around with her."

He hears no response, but the sound of the moving bush is still very clear. He pulls up his zip quickly, and turns around, "Craig, is that you, buddy?"

Abruptly the music stops, and complete silence prevails. He takes a step forward, with low confidence. "Guys, not funny." He peaks in the direction of the sound, but before he can take another step, the sounds come from behind him. Upon looking, there's nothing that he sees.

He begins approaching the camp, hoping to get there safe and sound. As he gets closer, he's surprised by the silence. The music had died out earlier, but why couldn't he hear anything? It appears as if no one was there in the woods but him alone.

As he gets closer, he sees the campfire vacant. He wonders if the rest had called it a night. The silence is alarming, but he wants to believe that nothing is out of the ordinary. Not once does he turn behind, convincing himself against the fear that is fueling his consciousness.

He looks at the camps, which seem quiet. "Guys," he yells desperately hoping for a response. The four camps are set up in a kind of a plus. He walks into the one he and Charlotte are sharing. He peaks inside and finds her lying down, covered in a blanket. He takes a step behind and decides to peak into Craig's camp. He was the only one who did not have a partner, so there wasn't much privacy he'd be breaching. He looks inside and finds the camp empty. By now, he knows something is not right. He just hopes his intuitions are leading him in false directions.

Hoping his friends were picking up on him, he decided to get into his camp and lay next to Charlotte. He has to get through the night. He gets inside and slips inside the blanket. His chest now faces her back. He kisses Charlotte on the forehead, but she does not respond

As fear is taking a toll on him, he decides to search for distractions. He gently uses his hand to caress

Charlotte's body. He feels his palm against her stomach, making his way up there her breasts while constantly kissing her cheeks. "Babes, not gonna let you sleep."

Charlotte lays response less, "you ignoring me?" Aron asks out of frustration. "Are you sweating?" He pulls his hand out of her shirt in frustration, to forcefully turn her around. As soon as he does, he notices his left hand is covered in blood. He immediately pushes away. Tears start rolling down his cheeks. He looks at her in despair and then looks at his own hand.

His cries get louder with each passing breath. Then, all of a sudden, he begins to gather himself, as he wipes the countless tears streaming from his eyes. He realizes he needs to check on the others. With shivering hands, he unzips the side pocket of his traveler's bag. He pulls out the Swiss knife. He slides it in his pocket and hurries his way out.

He runs into Tim and Sara's camp and does not find them there, although their shoes lie outside. He then revisits Craig's camp, and upon not finding him there, he finally moves toward the last camp, hoping to find Kate and Nick. As soon as he enters, he finds their bodies piled up, one on another, with fresh blood spilled all over. His heart stops for a moment. He pushes his way inside and looks at them in disbelief, crying even louder.

Drowning in fear and grief, he's pulled out of his thoughts by a hand he feels is placed on his shoulder. He's initially too afraid to look behind and stays put. He can see a shadow being cast in front of him.

His lips tremble as he speaks, "Pl… pl..plea..please..lett..lett. mee go. I won't tell anybody about it."

He hears a soft grunt of a giggle. "I swear… I swear, Oh God…I swear I will never speak of it. Please let me go."

The hand is lifted. Aron knows that he's not going to get any mercy, not after all that he has seen. He turns around in an attempt to escape, but before he can make a move, he receives a blow on his forehead. His head spins around as he loses his balance falling face off on the ground. He somehow pushes himself off the ground to seek escape. All he sees is a vivid image of a black man, holding a hammer. He crawls to make his way out of the camp and is allowed to do so.

He tries to get on his feet and fails in his first attempt. He makes another attempt, and although he manages to land his weight on his legs, he still struggles to balance. There comes another blow, this time the hammer strikes him on the back. He falls flat on the ground, feeling paralyzed.

A weird voice addresses him, "Gein says hello."

Unable to move Aron, rolls his eyes to see who is attacking him, but all he sees is a black spirit. The face is dark, and no part of it is visible. Maybe it's the loss of clarity in his vision, or maybe what he sees is in fact what there is.

He thinks of using the Swiss knife he has in his pocket in an attempt to attack the man dressed in black. His body gives up, but his mind refuses to give in. He, slowly, pulls the knife out.

Before he can take action, he's grabbed by the hair, as the voice speaks, "Ever killed a dead man?"

The voice begins laughing, horrifically. Aron feels his heart-stopping, but before he loses his breath consciously, he receives a final blow, crushing part of his skill. And there he lay, motionless.

CHAPTER 3
LET'S HIT THE ROAD

The clock ticker was mixed with the sound of gasps of breath as Mike and Lily felt each other's lips. From sharing seats on the couch, Lily was gradually shifting her weight from her spot to Mike's lap, while Mike was leaning back allowing Lily to get comfortable.

She loved the cologne he was wearing, but now the smell of his body was all she could sense. Her toes curled as she got on top, and Mike could no longer support his neck as it rested on the edge of the couch. Mike wanted to taste more and more of Lily, and her shoulders wrapped around his neck had made him vulnerable. This wasn't the first time they were kissing, but somehow it felt like they had never kissed this way before.

"Is the door locked," Mike pulled his lips away with force. It's not that she wasn't allowing him to get distant, but it was his own will that he had to oppose.

"No, and neither are we locking it," Lily said with her lips moving to the side and eye brows rising.

Mike's disappointment was evident as his hands loosened the grip of her waist and dropped to the sides now resting on her hips.

Lily leaned in closer to his right ear and whispered, "Let's save it for tonight." She bit his ear lobe and licked it gently with her tongue.

Mike closed his eyes and immediately pushed his fingers through her hair pulling her head back, and then running her lips into his. His one hand dropped and began feeling Lily's hips, his fingers trying to squeeze their way through the denim shorts she had put on. Suddenly, they were pulled out of their ecstasy as the bag lying next to Mike took a roll and landed on the ground. The two looked toward it in surprise to see what had happened and broke away in laughter. The fallen bag gave Mike the room to slip sideways on his back, and Lily was now lying over him.

Lily knew she couldn't resist much if Mike continued so she slowed down the curling of her tongue to the point where their lips were no longer intact. She then rests her head on his shoulder.

"What if the story of the woods was true?" Lily asked with concern in her eyes.

Mike adored her innocence, and played along, "What story?"

"You know what…. Is it worth the risk?" She added.

"Oh babes, people talk all kinds of shit. This is what makes it fun." Mike said caressing her hair, as his eyes were locked on the roof.

"But…I mean..forget it." She figured arguing wasn't going to be productive so preferred keeping her thoughts to herself. Lily wasn't someone who had a weak heart, but this did not mean she'd jump in a well to prove her strength. If it wasn't for Mike, she would've been just as skeptical as Jason.

"Let's say, worst comes worst. I'd grab my Swiss and stab the hell out of whatever tries to harm you. What do you say." He exclaimed with a smile of pride.

Lily straightened her head, with her chin digging into his chest. She smiled it off and locked her lips with his. Once again, the two of them began kissing wildly. This time around what had them stop was Mary's knock.

The first knock went unattended, which was followed by the next. Mary had been patient enough, but upon receiving no response she was left with no option but to push her way through the door.

"Ted is about to come, guys," Mary said in a loud voice to make sure she wasn't unheard.

Lily put her foot on the ground to ease her way back. Mike, too, sat up, pressing his fingers against his hair to get them back in shape.

"About is forever," Mike commented, which was more of him disapproving of the interruption than being asked to wait.

"Lily, please tell me you're done with packing," Mary questioned with a tone identical to that of a tired mother. Her role in the crew had somewhat been of the disciplinary, and since she always spoke of what was right, she wasn't usually argued with. The others often mumbled as spoiled brats, but this did not mean they wouldn't conform.

"Yes, Mom, almost done," Lily replied teasingly.

Mary mimicked like a fed-up mother in an accent that was not hers, "Get your asses out in 5." Her words were followed by a faint smile.

"You aren't here for goodbyes, isn't it?" Jason questioned with seriousness ridden all over his face.

Ted was seated in his truck. The 1998 Chevy hadn't been with Ted for long, but it was in good shape. The red exterior and black interior gave it a sporty look. The bull bar in the front and the power house of search lights he had recently installed made it a perfect ride for the adventure.

"Why else would I be here?" Ted responded with both hands on the wheel seemingly avoiding eye contact as he looked at him for an instance and straightened his head right after.

Jason was standing at the door of the truck with both his hands holding the door that had its windows dropped down.

"Hop in," Ted added.

Jason dropped down his head as if he knew where this conversation was heading. He took a step back, opened the door, and sat right next to him. Ted's hands were still resting on the steering wheel, and Jason sat just as his friend on the driving seat, staring into thin air.

"You know she'd be happy to see you!" Ted muttered. As soon as he finished his sentence, he changed his posture with his chest facing Jason.

"She won't be sad to not see me." Jason reprimanded.

"Dude, this is your chance. I mean who knows where we end up for our degrees? I might just be here in this truck, but it's not me that you should be worried about." Ted seemed more energetic now.

Jason grinned. It seemed as if he had an answer, but he kept it to himself.

"The big city and the big parties can wait. Mary cannot. What's so hard in there for your dumb head to understand," Ted said convincingly.

"Yes, I like her, but me going there isn't going to change much. So, if that's what you're here to sell, I reckon you save your time," Jason was unmoved.

"Did you for once tell her how you feel about her? For fuck's sake bro, you gotta tell her how you feel?" Ted insisted.

Jason flinched his eyes, and replied, "tell her what Ted? Tell her what?"

Ted passed a fake smile and took longer than a minute to reply, "All I'm saying is, I don't want you to regret not taking your chances. I know she likes you, and you're too stupid to see…You know what…you don't wanna come, then fucking don't come. She's better off with a guy who has the balls to confess his feelings."

"I don't want to make a fool out of myself."

"What makes you think you already aren't!"

"But…"

"No if's and buts, go inside, get your shit together, and come out with a bag in less than ten." Ted interrupted.

Jason stared at him, got out of the car, and turned around to walk back inside. Barely taking a couple of steps, he turned back, "You sure?"

"Go…" Ted exclaimed.

He turned around and went back inside to grab his stuff and join the crew.

Ted honked outside Mike's house, where the rest of them eagerly awaited his arrival. Mary was the first one to get down and was surprised to see Jason accompanying him.

"Gonna miss out on the uptown girls, huh!" Mary said while tossing her bag pack in the rear of the Chevy.

Jason made his way around her, "I figured they could wait."

Mary passed a smile in return. By now the rest of the crew had arrived and were loading the truck with their belongings. Lily high-fives Jason, and Mike gives him a tight hug. Ted tied down the bags together with the camps and asked everyone to jump in. It was time to head to the woods.

Ted accelerated with the gang buckled up. He switched on his stereo system and put on Careless Whisper by George Michael looking at Jason through the corner of his eye. Jason glared back and immediately had the track changed. He knew Ted was messing around with him.

The sun was set to disappear as the orange sky, was transitioning into grayish blue. They had stopped for fueling and were all set to drive for a longer spell. The GPS showed the location they intended to camp at to be a six hours drive. The first two hours had passed but the energy hadn't changed a bit.

The next stop Ted made was to change drivers. Although he wasn't very comfortable with letting others drive him around, he knew it was a long ride. He sure could take a few hours rest before arriving at the campsite and setting up the camps.

"Jason, you'll take the wheel?" Ted inquired as if he hadn't questioned but instructed.

Jason shook his head in approval and climbed the driver's side. As Ted was about to make his way to the front passenger seat, he was intervened by Mary. "I'll take this seat."

"All yours," Ted replied and winked at Jason, making sure Mary had her back on him.

Jason droves for the next three hours, which was until they arrived at the last town. The clock showed 11, and the GPS showed a five-mile offroad.

Jason stepped out to stretch his legs, while the others attended to nature's calling. Mary stayed with him.

"Can I ask you something," Mary asked in a soft tone.

Jason felt vulnerable as if she could see through him. He rested his back behind the rear passenger door shaking his head in agreement.

"What convinced you to stay?" Mary questioned with innocence in her eyes that was disguising her smartness.

"You," Jason instantly responded. He had gotten nervous and was regretting his answer. He added, "I mean who knows where we end up for our degrees."

As Jason finished the last part of the sentence, Lily and Ted returned from using the bathroom.

"Guys, I'm cold," Lily said folding her arms.

"I need to use the loo too," Mary said and headed to the bathroom.

Mike joined the rest and gripped Jason's shoulder.

"Does it look like people live here? I can barely see anybody here." Mike said with curiosity.

"At this time of the night, be glad you can't see anybody," Ted said with a chuckle.

The place was quiet, and the town seemed abandoned. The whirling wind and the empty streets were all there was to see. The houses seemed empty, but there were a few dim lights that were visible, which made their appearance even more spooky. Dust and debris seemed to cover most of the ground, while the gardens were unkempt appearing to be home to all kinds of wildlings.

There was one old man sitting beside the pump, who was dressed in a Janitor's outfit. He had long hair, but by the looks of it seemed like it hadn't been combed for days. His eye brows were just ass white as his hair, and the long nose gave him a furious look. Mike tried to communicate with him, but he did not seem interested. He just gave him an unwelcoming stare which was enough for Mike to know the conversation had ended before it even started.

"Oh boy, the story seems to have some weight. Look at this place, has anyone ever lived here in centuries," Jason stated.

"Well, that old man sitting in the corner tells you that

life exists here. It's just that we're here in the middle of the night," Ted replied.

The paint crumbled off the walls, and the only few cars parked seemed like they had been untouched for ages.

"Try asking the guy where can we get some snacks from?" Mary put forward her advice.

"Snacks? We got shit loads of them," Lily countered.

"I know, but at least, this will help you guys not shit in your pants if that is of any help," Mary grinned.

The rest of them smiled, but none found the courage to walk up to the man who was probably sitting fifteen yards away from them. Jason felt obliged to take Mary's suggestion and as he began to walk in the man's direction, Mary stopped him, "I think we should leave. I can't wait to reach our spot and settle down."

Jason didn't argue, Mary took the front seat, and Jason hoped behind with Mike and Lily. Ted took the driver's seat. They took the final right and began off-roading to reach their destination.

As they paved the way through dirt and patches of mud, darkness surrounded them. Ted switched on his search lights, and it did make it bright enough for them to see their track clearly. Other than that, it was all dark and gloomy. Since nothing else was visible besides what fell under the rays of the truck light, they kept their eyes focused on what they could see.

"The map shows we're almost here. Pull over," Mary said grabbing everyone's attention. The boys pulled out the stuff laying in the open trunk, and together the five of them, walked a few yards to reach a spot they found suitable.

Relying on their flashlights they set up their camps, ignoring the possibilities the dark could hold. After all, this is what they had signed up for, and even though horror seemed to accompany them, none of them spoke of it.

The smell of mud and distinct sounds of insects were prominent, but they didn't pay much heed to it and got to work. The rustling sound of the leaves made it difficult for them to decipher between the movement of the wind from that of a living creature. Each other's company and the silly jokes made everything sufferable.

Ted and Jason were sharing camps and so were Mike and Lily. Mary was going to have the camp to herself, which she knew was going to be a bit challenging in the last hours of darkness. It was a few more hours before sunlight peaked through, but it had been a long day for the gang. They knew they'd crash way before the early morning rays revealed.

"Time for beers," Jason exclaimed. He had waited quite long for the booze, something which was a task for him on his own. While on the road, none of them wanted to get too high on liquor and the cans were packed along with the bag packs. Mike, Ted, and Mary were motivated to start the fire, as even in their jackets and hoodies, they weren't able to combat the cold.

As soon as the fire was started, they lay mats around it and settled down to take some heat. By then Jason had passed them beers, and the crew celebrated their first night.

"Guys, I'm too tired to stick around, I'm crashing," Ted announced and made his way into the camp he was to share with Jason. Mary pulled out her guitar and began singing her favorite Taylor Swift song "Love Story." Although Jason did not like Taylor Swift one bit, with Mary singing it, he could've listened to it all night. Mike and Lily began dancing.

Jason adored Mary in serenity and Mary could somehow see it in his glittery eyes. The flashlights were switched off and the bonfire was the only source of light. Mike leaned in to kiss Lily. Suddenly they felt something had run past them.

"Did you see that?" Mary said putting her guitar aside. Mike and Lily looked just as surprised as they too had noticed a weird sound.

"I hope it's not tigers," Jason said worryingly.

Mike slowly walked away from Lily and went inside his camp saying, "We should keep the gun close, just in case."

"Should I wake Ted," Jason questioned in doubt.

"No, let him sleep. Maybe it's the wind." Mary suggested.

"What if it's not?" Jason fired back.

"Calm down, Jason. We're in the woods. It's home to many species, so even if there's a bear or a Jackal, one bullet is all that it'll take." Lily supported Mary. Mike was now out with his gun.

"Your turn," Mary switched the subject of discussion as she picked back her guitar.

"What?" Jason had no idea what she meant.

"I'll play and you'll sing," Mary clarified.

"My voice…." Jason tried to respond.

"Song?" Mary wasn't taking no for an answer.

"More than words. Know that song?" Jason replied.

"I knew you'd pick it," Mary responded and began playing the soft chords for him to sing. Jason had a beautiful voice, and regardless of the compliments he received, he never took his singing skills seriously.

Jason began humming, as Mike and Lily sat on the other side of the fire.

What would you do
If my heart was torn in two
More than words to show you feel
That your love for me is real

Mary had her eyes frozen at Jason while he sang with emotion. Mike and Lily moved to the strumming of the chords. After the song was over, they all went inside their camps, leaving the fire out on its own. Jason wished he'd join Mary, but figured it'd be too soon to make a move. He could just wait for the next night to come, hoping it to be more fulfilling. The four of them had forgotten about the weird noise, or so they were pretending.

CHAPTER 4
CABIN IN THE WOODS

The morning rays made the jungle look like a completely different place. The moon had taken away horror with it, and the sound of the clicks of the bats was replaced with the pleasant chirping of the birds.

The crew had slept well the previous night after a long drive and exhaustive setup. The booze needed some time to flush out of their system, but it did not take them longer than 8 when the sun welcomed them on one of the brightest mornings in the woods.

Ted was enjoying the fruit salad that he had freshly made with the fruits they had brought. It was only bananas, apples, and oranges. He was the first one to get up, maybe because he was the first one to sleep. Mary was the next to wake up, and she started her day with Croissants stuffed with cheese. Soon the rest were up, and the campsite had come to full life.

Jason was the last one to get up, which probably was because he was the last one to sleep, or maybe it was due to the unlimited number of cans he had consumed. He splashed some water on his face and walked straight toward Ted without interacting much with the lot while the whole crew curiously observed his motion. He grabbed the bowl Ted was holding and took a spot right next to him as he began munching on it. It was a funny sight and spread smiles around everyone's faces.

"I'll be back in a while; I need to digest some of this cheese," Mary said as she lit a cigarette and tossed the pack to where Mike was sitting; it was where she had picked it up from.

"Is it some kind of meditation?" Ted said and then chuckled.

"I never said I needed to be alone," Mary replied, looking at Ted and then Jason. As she turned around and took a few steps, Ted slid to his right with some force, deliberately colliding into Jason. The spoon slipped out of Jason's hand as he looked at Ted's expression, telling him to join her.

Jason put the bowl on the side, grabbed a beer, and took quick steps to get to her. Mary was still close. By the time he got to her, the camp was distant enough for their conversation to be heard.

"Mind if I join," Jason asked.

"Yes," Mary replied with a poker face.

Jason was startled, and his expression showed. Before he could say a word or react, Mary broke into laughter, and so did he.

The next five minutes of the walk were silent. Mary seemed to be consumed by the woods as if there was nothing in her mind. On the other hand, he was constantly thinking of subjects that would lead to an interesting conversation.

"Got smokes?" she spoke.

"You never smoked this much," Jason pulled out the pack from his back pocket.

Mary smiled, "There's a lot of fresh air out here. It's ok to smoke here." She laughed at presenting the theory.

"Hey, look there….to the right?" You see that" Jason said excitedly.

"Woah, looks like something," Mary was just as amazed.

Jason began walking toward it, and as they got fairly

closer, they were fascinated to see a cabin in the middle of nowhere.

"Careful," Mary cautioned him out of concern. He turned back to look at her with a smile. They were now five yards away when Jason stopped, and so did Mary as she was right behind her. He took a deep sigh, staring at the cabin. He swung his head in the direction of the cabin, stating his intentions through his expressions. She didn't mind the idea and signaled back with a yes.

As he advanced toward the cabin, he stepped on the pile of leaves, and all hell broke loose. He had stepped on a trap that tied around his leg and pulled it as soon as his foot landed on it. Mary rushed toward him, taking a longer route, avoiding the leaves to ensure she did not fall prey to another trap.

"My leg…..hurts a lot," Jason cried out.

"I am coming, I'm coming, hold on," Mary responded.

As soon as she got to him, she took out the lighter she had in her pocket and burned the rope to free his leg. She noticed his foot was bleeding. "Ok, so Jason, count to three," she helped him stand as he put most of his weight on the unhurt leg. He put his arm around her shoulder and slowly hopped toward their campsite with her support.

She could sense the pain and hear him moan as they made their way to their safe zone, where their friends were.

"I hope we're headed in the right direction."

"We're almost there," Mary answered with certainty in her voice. She was secretly hoping she remembered the route correctly. Finally, they got to a point where Ted's Chevy was visible. As soon as they got close enough to be heard, Mary yelled, "Guys....need help!"

Mike and Ted were playing chess, and Lily was their only audience. She immediately heard Mary's voice and alerted the boys. Instantly, the three of them were on their feet and sprinted toward Mary and Jason.

Upon seeing them approaching, Mary rested him on the ground and bent over, pressing her palms over her elbows. The walk had exhausted her.

"That does not look nice," Ted said as he grabbed him by his shoulders, lifting him up. Mike lifted him from his feet, "We got you, buddy!"

Lily stared at Mary for answers as she passed the water bottle she was holding. Mary took a few sips and, without saying anything, followed the boys. Lily didn't bother her much and followed after her.

"Lay him here. Who was responsible for the first aid?" Mike inquired.

Mary responded to the call, went inside her camp, and brought the first aid camp. The crew asked what had happened, and she explained the instance in detail. She told them about the abandoned cabin. Mike disagreed with it being abandoned because there wouldn't be a mantrap placed there if it was. They debated a bit on it, and everyone shared their opinion until the topic did not seem any more interesting.

Jason seemed in immense pain and just kept on lying flat on the ground. They didn't ask a lot of questions to him either. He needed rest.

As dawn approached dusk, the crew settled down in the campsite. There was tension as Ted grilled the chicken they had brought with them. They were hoping it hadn't rotten, but Ted said he had it prepared in a way that it would last a few days. The painkillers, by then, had brought Jason into a more relaxing position. Mary covered him with her blanket and squeezed herself in. Soft music was playing, which seemed like Mike's playlist.

"I think we should leave in the morning," Lily shared her opinion.

Mike nodded, and Ted remained silent, centering his attention to the chicken he was roasting.

"The cut is not that deep. The pain is not too bad. I don't think there's one good reason for us to leave."

"Buddy, I think Lily's right. You came here for us, and we love you for that, and we can leave with you without any regrets." Ted said as he walked up to him to pass him the freshly cooked piece of chicken.

"I am fine. If I wasn't I'd tell you guys. I want this trip to be special. I want this trip to be long." Jason argued.

"We'll do something else. Maybe go to Vegas with you," Mike suggested.

"I don't want to go to Vegas. I want to be here with you guys. I am not leaving, and I'm not gonna let any of you leave." Jason was unconvinced.

"Ok, but I'm going there tomorrow and seeing what the fuck is up with the traps. Maybe it's gold in there," Ted answered back, and the rest laughed and agreed to go with him.

The next morning the crew left for the cabin with Mary leading them to show them where it was. Mike kept his gun and Swiss knife with him, while Lily even kept her pepper spray. Once they reached the cabin, Mary gave a short speech, which was basically asking everyone to be cautious. Ted led the way as he used his stick to ensure he didn't step on something wrong. The rest followed.

Once they got close to the camp, they decided to break in. Mary knocked first to make sure no one was inside. Mike pushed open the door and climbed inside, and Mary, Ted, and Lily joined him, respectively.

The cabin was made of rustic logs of wood, and it was very small, as it appeared from the outside. It had a bed on one corner and a locked door on the other end. It was messy, and the passage was filled with luggage that was covered in dust, with only enough space for a person to walk. The dishes were lying in the only sink, which was the first thing you saw upon entering. Nothing in the log made it look like anybody lived there besides the dirty dishes. It had a pungent smell, which was a mixture of damp wood and fresh meat.

Lily was the first one to exit as she couldn't take the smell. Mary and Mike got out next, and Ted was the last one to exit.

"What do you say, someone lives here?" Mary questioned.

"Looks like…We should start going through the stuff that's in there," as Mike completed, the loud growls of a dog were heard. "Hurry, I think he's back."

As they started to move away, they noticed an angry rottweiler staring at them. Ted used his stick to scare him away, but he kept barking with aggression. Mary picked up a stone to throw at him if he attacked. The dog was closing in as they were slowly moving back. As the dog jumped toward them, Ted hit him with the stick that pushed it back. Mary threw a stone targeting it, although she missed the target, it sent the dog back a few yards. It was enough for the crew to make its way away safely.

As they wandered in the woods, making their way back to the campsite, a lake caught their attention. It had been a couple of days since they had taken a bath. Lily ran toward the lake without seeking anyone's approval. She took off her clothes and jumped right in, and so did Mike, Ted, and Mary.

Meanwhile, Jason spent time with a novel that Mary had given her. It was "The Host" by Stephanie Meyer. Jason enjoyed reading every now and then, but reading in the woods was a totally different experience. It was very peaceful. He would have enjoyed reading page after page if he wasn't interrupted by a tough voice.

"What you reading?" the man questioned right away.

"Hello, looking for someone?" Jason responded as he closed the book.

"No, just saw your leg; thought I'd ask if you were doing ok," the man replied.

Jason was getting uncomfortable. The man had a long hair. He was wearing a cap, but he could see the man had long hair that was tied up to the back. He had that southern drawl in his accent.

"I am, thank you for asking."

"What happened, though? Crossed the line you shouldn't have?" he ended with a giggle as if he found his question quite funny.

"Haha, no, just tripped over," Jason preferred keeping his responses brief as he answered with a fake laugh.

"How many ya'll out here?" he fired back with another question. From his appearance, he looked like a lumberjack.

"It's me and a few friends."

"A few too many or a few too less," the man laughed again.

This time Jason just smiled, hoping it was the end of the conversation and that the man would walk away.

"You know the woods can be a dangerous place," he took a pause and walked a couple of steps closer. He was still distant from the campsite and had to communicate loudly.

"All kinds of animals here. Wild dogs…. wolves, bears…..snakes," his voice had a kind of sharpness in it that was making Jason very uncomfortable. Jason didn't become an active participant in the conversation. He just kept listening.

"You know, what I'm most scared of," he did not care about Jason's lack of interest.

"Humans," he took a long pause without any expression on his face. A look that made Jason want to run away, and had his foot been in good shape, he might not have given a second thought to the matter. Then suddenly the man began laughing loudly.

"I'll push off, just be careful here, kid; the woods are not just fun and games. It's the wild; it can get wild." This time he did not laugh but just dabbed his hat as a goodbye.

Watching the man walk away was very relieving. He put on his headphones and lay flat, hoping to forget the encounter. The painkillers had made him lousy, and within a few minutes, he was asleep.

As his eyes opened, he looked around to see if his friends were back, but no one seemed to be there. He looked at his phone to see how long he had been asleep. It turned out he had been sleeping for a bit over half an hour. He went through his playlist and selected another song, hoping it would keep his thoughts from wandering around the horrors of the woods.

Consumed in the music, he stared into the sky, which was partially visibly, partially covered by the wildly grown branches of the trees. He thought of how Mary helped him get back. He was admiring her in any possible way that he could, and it could be seen through the smile that had captured his face. As the song ended and silence prevailed for a brief moment, he heard a sound.

He immediately disconnected his earphones and looked around to see if he had company. He knew if it was someone from the crew, they would come up straight to him and ask him how he was doing. 'I should call Ted," he murmured as he dialed Ted's number. No one answered.

"Hello," he hoped for an answer back.

"Anybody here?" Nobody responded.

He gathered all the strength that he could, and putting all his weight on one leg; he tried to gain his balance. He jumped a few steps to look around, but since he had been lying down all day, he kind of felt dizzy.

He feared it was the man who was there earlier. He could be there to steal away stuff, or maybe it was someone else. As he rubbed his hand around his eyes and hair to feel less drowsy, suddenly he was hit on the back of his head so intensely that he fainted right away.

CHAPTER 5
CALL JASON

The weather was warm, but the water was cool. They had a great time swimming. Mike did joke around every now and then about a whale that was in the lake, but they didn't even get a chance to see any fish. They screamed and enjoyed themselves to the fullest, and the echoes of their sound showed how they were all alone in the woods.

"I'm cold," Lily exclaimed as soon as she stepped out. She dressed uncomfortably. The dry clothes and the wet body made her want to change instantly, but she couldn't do it until they reached the camp where she had more of her clothes.

"It was your idea," Mary responded with a giggle. Ted and Mike sat on their heels, sitting with their arms crossed. They wanted to dry themselves as much as they could before they put on what they had.

"Have we taken too long? Jason would be all worried?" Mary said in a soft voice. It seemed like a question she had asked herself.

"He'll be doing fine. Nice to see that you're worried," Ted added with a deeply meaningful expression.

Mary cleared her throat; he had caught her off guard. She replied, "I'd just be as worried for any of us."

"I know," Ted gave a wide smile. He got on his feet to pull up his pants. He was already wearing his shirt, so it barely took him a moment. He then wore his watch and passed Mary her bag. "My phone."

Mary searched through her bag and passed him his cell phone. He grabbed and unlocked it. The rest were ensuring they had gathered their belongings when Ted demanded their attention. "Jason's texted…he tried calling too, got a couple of missed calls."

"What's he saying?" Mike inquired.

"Well, he says…." Ted pauses, running his eyes over the entire message again, wondering if he wasn't reading it right. His expressions showed he was surprised. "He said, *I'm going to the nearest town. Gotta get some painkillers.*"

"That's so unlike Jason," Mary raised her concerns. "He could barely walk; I'm not sure if he should be driving," Mary added.

Ted was just as worried as the rest, but he figured raising concerns was only going to add to the panic already created. "I just hope he brings back my truck in one piece," Ted commented, trying to lighten the mood, but to no avail.

Mary lit a cigarette, took a few puffs, and passed into Ted. "Let's go; it'll take some time to get back."

"Don't worry, he'll be fine," Ted said in a low voice. Mike and Lily were in the middle of a brief kiss, so they didn't listen. Mary didn't retaliate. She just nodded hopefully.

The crew set to walk back in the direction of the campsite. As they walked away from the lake, Mike suggested that they take a shorter route as he could see on his GPS. It did involve some trekking, but it was shorter. Mary wasn't entirely comfortable with the idea, but she didn't want to make her concerns more prominent. When she did not see anyone else disagreeing, she didn't disagree either.

After a good seven-minute walk, they could see from a distance that they were closing in on the top of a hill. As they got there, they looked down to see a campsite that wasn't theirs.

"Don't people take their camps and stuff with them," Lily said out of fear.

"Maybe they left beers and tuna too," Mike attempted to comfort her.

"Eww, we're not gonna take the tuna," Lily answered back.

"For any of that, we'll have to make our way down the hill, and then you look at the elevation there." He pointed in the distance, "We'll have to climb back." So, it isn't going to be easy to carry a lot of stuff."

"Well, they brought it here," Mike argued.

"They did," Ted said to put an end to the pointless discussion. They were arguing over stuff they didn't even know if or not existed. Mary preferred staying out of the argument and was the first one to make her way down. "Just be careful," she said as she watchfully stepped on hard rocks to ensure she didn't slip. It was a lot of trekking, but they still had to be careful. They didn't want another one of them injured.

Ted was the first one to reach the end of it. He had done plenty of hiking and trekking, so the small little hike wasn't much of a challenge for him. Mike was the fittest, but he was guiding Lily and lending her a hand where required. Mary, Mike, and Lily almost got down together.

"Let's see what we have here." Mike seemed excited. The campsite was clearly visible, but they hadn't reached close enough yet.

"I just hope another dog doesn't come chasing," Mary said as the rest smiled.

The campsite was larger than theirs. It had seven camps. Each used to be white, but the dust had turned it into brown. In the middle of it was the fire area, which had nothing but ashes. All the camps were closed, and there were empty cans lying around. None spoke a word; they all looked around in surprise; something about it did not seem right.

"Hey, look at this," Mike said, pulling something out of the pile of dirt. "Somebody forgot their bag."

"He's not gonna come back looking for it," Mary said as she began to get closer to Mike, who was now unzipping the green bag covered in dirt. It had a pair of jeans, a T-shirt, some rotten nuts, and a few pills. It had a few blank papers in there too.

They opened the first camp and saw nothing in there besides the camping cot in place. Lily yelled as she and Mike opened the next. Ted and Mary rushed immediately to where she and Mike were. The other camp had its walls covered with splashes of a color that seemed like blood.

"Maybe, it's not what you think," Although Ted thought exactly like the rest of them did, he tried to believe it was something else.

"Like, what? They were slaughtering chickens in there to roast them for dinner," Mike replied in a sarcastic voice.

"Let's see the next," Ted insisted. He moved toward the third camp. The third camp had similar splashes, but it wasn't only the walls; the foam sheets lying around were also colored dark orange. It seemed that it was blood, and it had dried. It had a couple of bags piled up in one corner, but they decided to leave them untouched.

Right outside the camp was a set of earphones lying on the ground, next to a book. The book was covered in dirt, as was the rest of everything. Nothing in the book was readable, and the earphones also seemed in terrible shape.

Mike proceeded toward the fourth camp as Ted approached the fifth. Mike's camp had poker chips split into two halves and cards placed. It was evident that the last time someone was in the camp, they were playing poker.

The fifth camp had a bag lying at the entrance. Ted and Mary entered the camp. Ted said, "You look at the pattern on the foam."

"Yes, what does it look like," Mary asked innocently.

"What does it look like to you?" Ted made eye contact, telling her in a way that what she had in mind was indeed what it was. It was apparent that someone was dragged out as he or she tried to grab the foam. There was a stretch of marks on the nails.

"I don't know," Mary responded and turned around to exit.

"Guys, I'm freaking out," Lily blurted out, and instantly tears welled up in her eyes. Mike gave her a side hug but didn't say much. The sight was indeed horrific, and it had scared all four of them. Ted and Mary also lacked any words to comfort her. It was obvious that the campers did not get an opportunity to clean up their stuff when they were struck with an unexpected event. No matter how much they wanted to think otherwise, they couldn't. It added up in one way only – catastrophe.

"Let's get back before it's too late," Mary's voice was weak as she rubbed Lily's back in an attempt to comfort her.

The four made them away from the campsite, covered the short trek uphill, and went. Silence prevailed throughout the short journey as each thought of what could have happened to the camp. They had the horror story they had heard while planning the trip in the back of their mind. None confessed, but deep down, each of them had started believing it to be true.

Mary had more on her mind besides the abandoned campsite. She was worried about Jason. She kept thinking of how he never wanted to join them, and he had only come because of her. Ted had not shared the conversation he had with Jason with her. Nor did Jason confess to her, but she knew. She didn't need anyone to tell her how Jason felt about her. She could see it in her eyes.

She should have stayed there with him. She should have been more careful. The thought of not finding him there upon their return was very discomforting. The abandoned campsite had made them extremely worried for him.

"I can't see my truck," Ted commented as they closed in.

"He might have parked in on the other side," Mike commented.

"How can you be so sure that he took the truck? Was he in good enough shape to drive?" Lily tossed panic-ridden questions, and the three of them waited for the other to respond.

Finally, Ted spoke, "I can't see my truck. I can only hope he has taken it and not anybody else."

Lily realized what she said didn't make a lot of sense. Mary sprinted toward the camp, yelling Jason's name. The rest do the same but try calling it out in different directions. Upon reaching the campsite, they do not find him anywhere, and neither do they find Ted's truck. It sure didn't seem right, but all they could do was wait.

"He should have been more careful…I mean, we could have gone together." Mike said, resting his hand on his waist.

"That's how he is. Doesn't really think it through, does he?" Ted supported Mike's statement.

"You remember the time he slept over at my place without telling anyone at his house."

 "Oh boy, I got a call from his dad, and he seemed worried as fuck….and then, he called back, a couple of hours later to apologize, telling me he was at your place….I mean, what was he being sorry for? It wasn't his fault," Ted added.

"When he called me, and I told him that Jason was staying over, you know what they said," Mike completed looking at Lily and Mary, trying to make them a part of the conversation.

"What?" One of them replied.

"The next time I go out of town, I'm not telling him. You tell him that for me," Mike said in a made-up accent. He wasn't able to sound like Jason's dad, but he did manage to mimic the tone.

Ted walked over and grabbed a beer as the rest sat closer to the fire that was yet to be torched. "He'll be back soon, and when he does, Imma, kick his ass."

Mary wasn't expecting his sentence to end that way, and a small grin suddenly captured her face.

An hour passed as they eagerly waited for Jason's return. They kept talking about an instance where their missing friend's laid-back attitude landed him in trouble. The conversation shifted from Jason to other students of High School. Lily enjoyed gossiping, and that interest enabled her to make friendships with girls that kept her informed. The rest of them were surprised when she shared stories of Henry – the school playboy, and Samantha – the girl who slapped the principal.

Smokes and beers were what they had in abundance, and it suited them nicely as they waited for Jason. Another hour had passed, and the crew was beginning to become more worried for him now. Mary grabbed the book she had given Jason to read. She kept looking at the book while thinking about him.

Ever since the trip had started, things had become quite different between the two of them. There was a kind of tension that wasn't there before. It was happy tension. They were cautious and nervous yet wanted it to be no other way. They had different personalities. Jason's nervousness was evident, but Mary knew how to hide hers behind her confidence. She hadn't thought of him that way until the trip. The moment he got out of contact, she developed a fear of losing him. It was something she never thought she'd have for him.

"Nearest town?... Where could that be?" Ted began thinking out loud.

"The last town we saw seemed abandoned and creepy. I don't think he'd go there." Ted's words dragged Mary out of her thoughts, and she gave her insight on the matter.

"I checked on the GPS, that's the only town, and that's like really far, so it doesn't make a lot of sense to go there," Mike added.

"Maybe that town's not on the GPS," Lily valued in.

"I don't think so. Everything's there on the GPS."

"I've been trying his number for a while now. At least he could answer his phone and let us know he's safe," Mary said irritatingly.

"If he'd do that, would he be Jason," Mike joked.

"We don't even have the truck to drive around and look for him. We can't just walk around in miles to see where the nearest town is," Ted mumbled.

"See, the nearest town is hours distant, and if he's gone there, he's not coming anything soon. He'll probably return in the middle of the night, or maybe he might stay there the night, maybe sleep in the car, and leave for here in the morning. Which means he's not getting here before afternoon tomorrow," Mike explained.

"I hate to say it, but that's the only thing that makes sense," Ted agreed.

Mary wasn't happy with how it sounded, "It's not even dark yet, and you guys think he'd come after the sun goes down and then comes up again."

"Nearest town, Mary, the nearest town," Mike shrugged his shoulders.

Mary did not say a word in agreement but knew what Mike said made sense. They didn't have a car to do something about the situation. They were stuck there until he returned, so there was no other option besides waiting.

Mike's judgment had somewhat eased the waiting process. They were no longer impatiently looking around. They had somewhat agreed to the fact that Jason was going to take some time, and it was best to wait in peace instead of arguing or panicking.

CHAPTER 6

BLOOD AND BONES

Jason opened his eyes and began swinging his head both ways to counter the dizziness that had overburdened his consciousness. His eyes were flashing as the dim lightening of the room caught his attention. He was slowly getting back to his senses.

"Ted....Ted." He yelled with the little energy that he had left. "Why aren't you guys here? I need to go home," he murmured to himself as he began crying profusely. The tears blurred his vision, but he couldn't do anything to clear it. His hands were tied behind his back in what felt like chains. He did try to break free, but he sensed it was steel rubbing against his hand, and loosening its grip wasn't going to be easy.

He tried to bring his eyes in contact with his shoulders so that he could wipe away the tears. He had no success since his hands were not over his head but behind his back.

The smell of the room was terrible. It was as if someone had dipped his head in a pile of trash. Gradually, his vision cleared, and he began to take notice of his surroundings. It was a small room from what he could see, so there wasn't a lot for him to observe. The wall he faced was barely 4 feet distant from him, and a door was not visible. So, he assumed the door was right behind him. There was a wooden board placed right behind his head, which did not allow him to look over his shoulders.

On the right corner of the room were many cardboard boxes stacked up. The boxes weren't large in size, but they seemed covered in paint that had dripped on them. It was mostly red and grey. To the right of the boxes was a steel rack that had different tools placed on the first shelf. There were two more shelves below it, which were covered with dark blue plastic containers. He could see something inside them but couldn't really tell what it was.

On the left side, covering the corner of the wall he faced, was an open closet. It did not have any clothes hung on it but parachute raincoats that were all in blue. In the last part of it were three pairs of boots, all black. He suddenly looked back at the plastic containers and figured they had raincoats in them, similar to the ones that were hanged. It was very clear, nor was he very sure, but the entire outlook of the room was freaking him out.

"Hello, hello…..sir….. ma'am…ANYBODY!"

He then turned his head left. He could see a black couch that did not seem in good shape. Half of it was visible as the wooden board blocked his view of the other half. There was a low-voltage lightbulb hanging over his head. He couldn't see it because the wooden board restricted his head movement.

He began banging his head against the wooden board in frustration. Something needed to work, but nothing did. He did it for a good five minutes, but then his head began hurting terribly, so he had to give up.

He tried to pull himself down to rest on his feet since his already hurt leg caused a lot of pain. His hands were so awkwardly tied that they didn't allow him to bend his knees. The moment he'd try to put weight on his knees, he would feel the muscles in his forearm twisting with pain so intense that he'd have to straighten his knees right away. Besides the couch and a painting on the left side, there was nothing else that he could see. The painting was very weird. It showed a small kid holding a knife in one hand and some dead animal's skin in the other. The boy had his face painted with black and white marks on both his cheeks. It was scary.

The wall he faced had a clock, but it was not working, which he figured looking at the second's needle that hadn't moved an inch as long as he looked at it. The numbers on the dial had a bone texture which was white, and the wall clock was red in color. It also had a skull drawn in the center. The clock was very unusual, and looking at it, he felt even more uncomfortable.

He, again, tried to pull his hands with force, hoping he'd break away that would allow him to escape. With gasping and grinding his teeth, he put in all the force that he could, but nothing worked out. The room was dark, and it was hard for him to tell whether it was daytime or nighttime. Tears welled up in his eyes again. He hadn't eaten anything since he had opened his eyes. His throat was dry, and his body had used all the energy that he had. His eyes eventually won against fear, and he fainted.

Footsteps woke him up that were very loud on the wooden floor. He instantly pled, "Hello….Sir….Please help me….I….I need to go. Please."

The sound of the footsteps remained unchanged, and he received no response. It appeared someone was walking in a pattern. The sound got louder when the person got closer and became fainter when the person walked in the direction opposite of him. The room now smelled miserable. It seemed like dead animals were stored in those cardboard boxes. It smelled like fresh blood. The room stank the moment he had woken up, but the smell had become far more pungent as if the source of the smell was covered before, and now it was put out in the open.

Jason felt like vomiting, and he even tried, but since there wasn't anything, he had consumed for hours, he was unable to do so. He began breathing wildly as the smell seemed unmanageable. He began coughing and shook his shoulders widely to get rid of the nauseousness caused by the air of the fetid room.

The sound of the footsteps went away, but only for a brief moment. The footsteps got louder, and finally, a man walked past him straight to the open closet, tossing something inside it. He couldn't see or tell what it was. Jason had his eyes fixated on him. Still facing in the same direction as Jason, he ran his fingers through his hair and turned around. The way he looked at him, Jason felt numb. His body slowly began to shiver as his gulps of breath intensified.

"What….what do you want?" Jason exclaimed.

The man began walking toward him, and right when he stood in his face, he replaced his angry expression with a smile – a smile that was even scarier than his serious look. The man's teeth were in terrible shape. He had no facial her but a deep scar on different areas of his face. The scar on the left cheek appeared to be the deepest. His eyes were pear-shaped, and the rest of his face was hard-featured. If there was any hope of mercy left in Jason, it went away with the smile.

He switched back to his serious expression as he instantly got rid of his spile. He placed his index finger on his mouth, indicating Jason not to utter a word. Jason was never the strongest of people, and the past couple of hours were hell for him. He had his eyes closed by now because the sight of the man was indeed quite horrific.

The man got behind Jason, unchained his one hand, and tied it to a wooden bar that was a couple of feet high. This made Jason stretch, and it hurt, but he had lost any willpower to rebel against the huge monstrous man.

"What have I done to harm you?" Jason's voice had softened a great deal.

The man did not respond, and from how it sounded, it felt like he had left. Jason was devastated. He began thinking of his mother. He could see her very clearly as if she was standing right in front of him. Her long black hair was loved by many, and she did put in a lot of effort to maintain them. On his left, he saw his father. He closed his eyes, and the vision continued. He felt hallucinated.

His dad placed his hand on his mother's shoulder. His mom turned around and hugged him. Then his parents were joined by little Jason. He truly seemed like an angel. They were all dressed in white.

Then, he saw his mom hugging Mary. Mary looked so beautiful. She looked like a bride who was now looking at Jason, welcoming him in his arms. She seemed very happy. The next person he saw was Ted. From his expressions and body language, it seemed he was taking credit for Mary's presence in his life. He finally began walking closer to both of them standing there, and just when he was going to place his hand in hers, a splash of water pulled him back into reality.

The crazy man had splashed water from a bucket on his face, and he was back into the misery he had so hardly escaped. The reality was nothing like his imagination. He shook his head to dry away as much water as he could, and as he tried to develop a sense of the situation, he saw the man dressed in a leather coat. He could see one of the cardboard boxes was lying on the floor, half-opened. It was from where the ugly man had pulled it out. He seemed like a dead animal, and the smell in the room had gotten worse.

After looking through the rack that was on Jason's right, he found a cloth and stuffed Jason's mouth with it. Jason tried to resist and plea for his well-being, but the man pretended he couldn't hear a single word that he uttered. He used another piece of cloth that he had pulled out of the front pocket of his leather coat. He tied it stiffly around his arm, right where the shoulder ended. Jason was well aware that torture was coming his way and just hoped that this agony would end soon.

The man then went back to the rack and began searching through the tools. He put aside a saw and a hammer and resumed looking. Even though tears had reduced Jason's visibility, he still did not take his eyes off for a moment. After all, his fate was being decided. How could he not be attentive?

He then put the hammer and saw back, which was somewhat relieving for Jason. The man then stood up with an axe in his hand. He instantly freaked out. He tried using his legs to retaliate, but he noticed they were tied too. He didn't even know when that had happened.

The man stepped right in his face, with the axe resting on his shoulder. He gave the wide frightening smile again and then took a step back. He dropped the axe from his shoulder and used his other hand to strengthen his grip. He got in position, and transferring his weight from his back leg to his front, with one strong blow, he struck the axe right where he had tied the piece of cloth. It showed his practice and precision.

Blood spilled out of his arm like water out of a sprinkler. Jason's eyes bulged out with pain. He screamed his heart out, but the cloth in his mouth absorbed all his screams. He fainted instantly.

"Hello, hello, hello," Gain said with a wide smile. He then began whistling and walked to the other side of the room to bring a bucket. He placed the bucket right where blood was pouring out from. As the bucket filled, he constantly kept whistling as if he was doing so out of boredom.

As the bucket was half filled with blood, the stream of blood lost its pace; he put the bucket aside. He unchained his other hand and noticed a watch in it. He unbuckled the watch, had a good glance over it, and dropped it on the floor, kicking it away.

There was blood all over the floor. He picked up the bucket and put it on top of the rack. He then pulled out a plastic sheet from one of the plastic boxes on the rack and spread it on the floor. He then grabbed Jason by his only arm and dragged him into the center of the sheet. He then took the bucket away, and as he walked away from a few steps, he stopped in his tracks. He forgot something. He then turned back around and grabbed the chopped arm that was lying on the floor.

CHAPTER 7

TOWN OF THE DEAD

"Your crying isn't going to bring him back," Mike tried to comfort Lily, who had been profusely crying since she had woken up. The night was a very silent one. There was no music or stories which kept the night alive. Mike had woken up to sobs of Lily, and ever since he woke up, he had been trying to make her stop but had no success.

Mary and Ted woke up shortly after, and the two were just as concerned for Jason. Mary had tears in her eyes, but she wasn't willing to break into tears. She knew it was important for her to hold herself together, as it still seemed like a long quest to get back out of place safely and soundly.

They waited until the afternoon, but there was still no

sign of Jason's return, and something else had to be done besides waiting for him.

"Guys, get your stuff together," Ted broke his silence. A couple of times, he did think of saying something comforting to Lily to ease up her tears, but he just failed to find any words. Deep down, he was just as scared as Lily, but the only difference was that his eyes weren't teary.

Lily stopped crying and froze her eyes on Ted. Mike seconded, "We don't have a ride, so it shouldn't take long."

"But Jason…" Mary's voice had grown weak, "we can't leave him like that."

"So you're staying," Mike had lost all his patience. He was already having a hard time dealing with Lily's tantrums, and he just couldn't take another one.

"Hey, buddy, easy there. We're all worried," Ted mediated the situation before it escalated. He placed his hand on Mary's shoulder, "Jason was my best friend, Mary, but what do we do? We have no contact with him. God knows if he's still alive or not. And if something bad has happened to him, we can't just sit here and wait to be next."

Mary did not utter a word. She shook her head, surrendering to their decision. She sat with her knees upright and her elbows resting on them. She pulled her head behind, facing the sky, and then rested her forehead on her arms. Lily immediately noticed the discomfort and approached Mary. She sat next to her and began rubbing her back. Within a few moments, Mary was all in tears.

Ted and Mike preferred not to interfere and began gathering their stuff. Lily helped Mary get on her feet, rubbing her head through her hair with her nails. Mary gave her a forced smile and, wiping the tears, began collecting her things. Lily did likewise.

Within a few minutes, the four of them had their backpacks on and began walking away from the camp. As Ted, Lily, and Mike proceeded to head away from the camp, Mary stopped, looked behind with a wholesome glance, and pulled out a cigarette from the pack she was holding. She lit the cigarette and took the first puff when Ted's voice addressed her, "Mary." She turned around and joined the rest.

"Where's the map?" Mike inquired.

Ted pressed his lips before he finally spoke, "In the truck."

Mike sighed in disappointment. "So which way?" he said, looking at Mary, and upon receiving no response, he diverted his attention toward Ted.

"I'd say we follow the lakeside," Ted suggested.

Mary spoke but not very pleasantly, "You still remember the course."

He knew she was disturbed, so Ted preferred keeping any puns to himself. He just shook his head negatively and began walking in the direction they had taken a few days ago. "I don't mind walking in any direction. If any of you want us to head in a different direction, I'm up for it," he said, strolling forward without looking ahead. Mike and Lily followed, and after a brief pause, so did Mary.

As the sun had come to its lowest point, the four felt they had no idea of where they had reached. They had been walking for hours, and their bodies direly needed a break.

"Guys, let's just take a break," Lily urged.

Although it was important to travel as much as they could during daylight, they all needed a few moments to straighten their legs. They were relying on hope and followed wheel tracks to ensure they were headed in the right direction. Lily found herself a tree to rest her back. Mike sat adjacent to her sharing the other side of the same tree. Ted sat on the ground with his legs spread wide. He was holding his knees, indicating the never-ending walk had caused some pain.

"I'll take a piss," Mary dropped her bag and headed a few yards into the woods. It took her a few moments to return. "Guys, I think you should see this."

Ted lifted his head and turned around to share his body weight on his shoulders and knees equally. Lily left her bag and headed to Mary. Mike grabbed his bag and Lily's and followed the ladies.

"What's that?" Lily asked, pointing toward the cravings on the tree.

"It seems like some sign language. This shit is ancient. I need to take a picture of this," Mike responded.

"Save your batteries," the power banks are almost dead, and there's no charging it.

"Not that ancient, I think," Ted responded to Mike's statement. "Look at this," he demanded the crew's attention from a few yards away.

"These bones aren't that old," Mike commented as he observed their texture, turning them over through his feet.

Yet again, Lily broke into tears. "We aren't going to make it out alive," she said while crying.

"No, babes, I'm right here with you. I'll take care of you," Mike immediately grabbed her by the shoulder and pulled her close.

"I think we should get going. We need a decent place to stay the night," Mary advised.

"Why the night? Let's just get out of here," Lily argued.

"I wish it were that easy. Let's just hope one night is all it will take," she said with affection placing her hand on Lily's face. It was important that she did not have her hopes high, especially when she was having a difficult time coping with the situation. Ted also noticed some skulls and pointed toward them through his eyes. Mary got closer and saw, but also she said, "Let's go." They didn't want to freak out Lily anymore, even though the three of them were freaking out themselves.

They head back on the wheel tracks. After walking for a mile, the sun had disappeared, and darkness covered the sky and everything around them. They had to find a place to spend the night, and they seemed nowhere near one. Suddenly they noticed a light approaching from a distance, "Guys, look who's here," Mike exclaimed.

The gang stood their ground and waited for the vehicle to get closer. The car lights got closer and closer, and their faces lit up with excitement. For some reason, they knew it was Jason. As the truck got close enough, they first realized it wasn't Ted's truck. The truck did not seem well maintained, and it was a 70's model.

The vehicle stopped, the engine stopped running, and a man stepped out, "You guys and girls were expecting someone?" The southern drawl in his accent was prominent.

"No, sir, we're just trying to find our way out of here," Ted replied.

"You telling me, you guys walked here all the day way to walk back," he ended with a wild giggle. None besides him found his statement funny.

"No, we've lost a friend. And….and our truck," Mike clarified.

"I'd buy you losing your friend, but not the truck. Had a fight, he took the truck with him?" the man giggled again.

"No, he was injured. He couldn't drive," Ted said.

Mary interrupted, "Let me explain." Mary went on to tell him what had happened to Jason and how he and the truck had disappeared. He heard the long tale and pretended to have believed them.

"I can take you guys to the nearest town, coz that's where I'm headed to," he said with an ugly smile. His teeth seemed out of place.

The crew looked at each other just to see if anyone disagreed. They had no options but to take the lift and consider it a blessing. It wasn't going to be an easy ride, they felt, but they got in.

The driver switched the ignition, and the truck's engine got running. Before driving the car, the man in his tough voice said, "The truck's old, like me, but it'll take you to Mars if that's where you want to go."

Ted took the front seat, and the rest sat in the back seat. The car smelled bad, but they had to pretend that they didn't find the smell abnormal. Ted found the silence very awkward, and so he spoke, "I'm Ted. And these are my friends – Mary, Lily, and Mike."

"Are we too late for introductions? We're close to conclusions now," the man replied and then began laughing. The crew found the man very lame, and most of what he said didn't make a lot of sense.

"Your good name, sir," Ted inquired.

"People who live in the woods don't need names. I used to have one. Sam, I believe," the man answered without laughing.

Ted figured it was best to keep his mouth shut instead of receiving answers that apparently made the ride worse. After a long silent ride, the car pulled into a town that seemed similar to the one they had stopped by when they were heading to the woods.

He pulled in front of a house that seemed haunted from the outside. Ted turned behind to look at his friends and then turned straight.

"This is where the old man lives," the man broke the silence.

"Who?" Lily was quick to ask.

"The old man who's with you in the car," the man replied.

"How do we get to the nearest town from here," Mary inquired.

"Nearest town isn't that near, girl. Be my guest for the night, and I'll get you guys to the town tomorrow," the man welcomed them with looks that weren't very welcoming.

The man gets out of the truck and leaves the four inside to exchange words.

"I am not staying here. The man looks creepy," Lily objected.

"Doesn't look like anyone lives here. What does this man do for a living? Why does he live alone in this abandoned town." Mary fired questions.

"What do we do? We ask him which direction the town is in and keep walking towards it. I bet wolves and bears will offer us company along the route," Ted raised his concerns.

Mike remained silent. He knew what Ted said made perfect sense. Although the town seemed abandoned by any living creature, let alone humans, they couldn't do anything but stay.

"Let's just wait till morning," he exclaimed, "besides, I can't rely on granola bars anymore. One good meal is needed."

Lily and Mary knew that arguing at this point wasn't going to be of any gain. They needed a roof, and this man was offering them one. The rest got out of the car as the man stood by the entrance. As he noticed them approaching the house, he gestured for them to get inside.

Gein was wearing his apron and whistling as he began chopping the corpse into pieces. He knew the drill. He took off the skin from the body and cut the body into four pieces. He wrapped the other three pieces with a plastic sheet and began chopping the last piece. He cut the meat into small boneless pieces and put them in a bowl. He then took the bowl with him to the kitchen.

He put half of the bowl in a frying pan and began cooking it in red sauce. He added some salt and pepper as he covered the saucepan for the meat to be deeply cooked. He then removed the lid he had placed on the pan, and the sauce dried up. He took another cup from the bucket that was placed in a bucket next to his feet.

It was the same bucket that he had used to collect Jason's blood. It was, in fact, blood and not any sauce that he was using to cook the meat. As he stirred through the saucepan, he took a pause, taking a sip from a glass of wine that was placed next to the stove.

It did seem like he had long awaited this dinner, and he sure was going to enjoy it.

The trucker offered them two rooms, both of which were on the opposite extremes of the house. Lily and Mike went to the room that was on the left side of the entrance. Ted and Mary took the one that was on the right. Dirt seemed to have settled on the walls and had lamps on them that didn't glow very brightly.

Mike and Lily were kissing in their room when a knock diverted their attention. "I'll get it," Mike commented.

He opened the door and found the trucker standing outside. "Dinner's ready," he said with a creepy smile.

"Will be out in a minute," Mike said and closed the door.

Mary was sitting on one edge of the bed, while Ted was sitting on the other. Upon hearing the door knock, Ted moved toward the door and found the trucker who asked them to join him for dinner.

Ted is around to call Mary, and she instantly gets on her feet. As they follow the trucker toward the dining room, Mike and Lily step out of their room and join them. The five of them find seats, as the pot with the food is already placed. The man removes the lid of the pot and generously asks them to serve themselves.

Lily was the last one to take out food on her plate when suddenly a pet dog came running toward the trucker. Ted recognized the dog, and his recognition kind of slipped out through his words, "This dog...." He spoke.

The trucker had his eyes frozen at him, wanting him to speak more. Ted realized the awkwardness and then clarified, "This dog looks very attached to it. What breed is it?" Ted pretended to act normally. Even though he knew it was the same dog that had chased them down at the cabin, they had broken into.

"The kind we can't kill," the trucker replied without any expressions. After taking a brief pause, he began laughing out loud. Ted fake laughed to not make the conversation any more awkward.

The rest pick Ted's lead and pretend not to recognize the dog even though all of them did. Mike is the next to speak, "You enjoy cooking?"

"Only when guests are over," he answered.

"I've eaten food across all states but never have had anything that tastes like this," Mike complimented.

Mary added to the conversation, "You've hunted this down? What is this anyway?"

"No, I don't do the hunting and killing. I had it cooked by a friend. He would have loved to meet you, but this time around, it's really late," he replied.

"And this is?" Mary reemphasized.

"This is…. delicious food," he ended with a laugh.

They hadn't eaten anything solid in days, so they enjoyed the meal without asking any further questions. The food did smell different, but being served in a town where apparently no one lived, was indeed quite fulfilling. They were somewhat relieved to know he had friends and that people lived there. They just needed the night to pass, hoping that the morning would be more happening and lively.

CHAPTER 8
MIKE IS MISSING

The night had gotten quiet. Silence prevailed inside the wooden house as the four were settled into two rooms. Mike and Lily took one room, while Ted and Mary occupied the other room. It had been a very long day, and the walk was tiring, to say the least. The long-awaited dinner had made them lazy, and finding a bed to crash upon was a satisfactory way to end the day.

"Do you think something bad has happened to Jason?" Lily inquired as her eyes wandered to different parts of the room that she had just entered.

Mike took off his shoes and jumped right in the middle of the bed. The bed made a squeaking sound as he put his entire weight on it. It showed the wood was old and weak. He lifted his head up to make sure he didn't fall, and even if he did, this gesture wasn't going to save him. He said, "Who knows? I just hope he had chickened out and drove away out of fear?"

"I'd kill him if he'd done that. And well, he'd never do that," she replied, sitting on the bed and taking off her boots, having her back against Mike.

Mike slipped his hand under her shirt to caress her body as he said, "I just hope he's fine, even if it means taking away the truck with him." There was sorrow in his voice.

Lily was done removing her shoes, and pulling off her shirt, she lay down on her stomach extending her knee to Mike's lap. She kissed his forehead and rested her head on his shoulder. She wished for the same.

Meanwhile, Mary and Ted were trying to settle in the other room. Mary was unpacking her backpack to find her pajamas while Ted had unbuttoned his shirt and sat on the only chair in the room. The part of the bed was covered with the stuff Mary had pulled out of her bag, including a pair of lipsticks, her small bag of make-up kit, her earphones, her charging cable, and a bar of half-eaten chocolate. She had pulled out a few clothes, too, that she kept in her lap. Ted got off the chair and picked up the half-eaten chocolate.

"Thanks for the dessert," he said as he took the first bite from the chocolate.

"Save some from me," Mary responded as she finally managed to pull out the pajamas from the bag. She got busy repacking the bag.

As he passed the rest of the chocolate to her, he added, "I'll sleep down here. You can take the bed," he said, pointing toward the floor with his head as he rubbed his hands on his jeans.

Mary remained silent for a moment having her eyes locked on him. It was evident that something was going through her mind. She was probably going to counter the offer in courtesy but then decided that she needed the bed. She only shook her head.

"I need to change," she said after a brief moment.

"Sure, the bathroom's right there in the middle," he responded.

"Ummm…can you like wait outside for a minute? I don't wanna go there," Mary said with a polite expression.

"Sure," Ted couldn't refuse. If he had to change, he'd ask the same of Mary, he thought to himself. The bathroom was in the middle of the passage that connected the two rooms. Even standing outside alone in the silence and darkness needed some courage, so asking her to go to the bathroom was indeed a bit too much to ask.

He went outside and looked around. The faint moonlight entering through the windows was making the scene even scarier, so he just hoped that a monster didn't come out from the dark to attack him.

It took Mary three long minutes to open the door. She was making her way to the bed as he entered and noticed that she had made his bed as well, however, on the floor.

"You did not have to do that," he said, scratching his head.

She smiled without saying anything. She laid down, covering herself with her blanket. She left the one in the room for Ted.

Ted sat back on the chair, shaking his right leg constantly. The movement of the leg created a noise that was of the wood.

"Can you stop that?" Mary said out of frustration.

"Yes, sure," he replied with a smile that Mary wasn't seeing.

"You sleeping?" Mike inquired.

"Mmm hmmm," Lily replied.

"Can I get a BJ?" he said with a chuckle.

Lily instantly hit his shoulder with her hand and the two burst out into laughter.

'You remember our first date?" she asked.

"Of course, the B&B Café," he said, swinging his head to the right to kiss her head that was still on his shoulder.

"You were so nervous," Lily now lifted her head and grabbed his cheek by her fingers, pulling them in awe.

"I didn't want to mess it up?"

"You know what dad said when you met him that day to pick me up?" she said, feeling his chest with her fingers.

"What?" Mike replied, staring at the roof.

"Girl, I would have asked him to take care of you, but it seems you'll have to take care of him. He said and laughed," she added.

"Did he literally say that?" he asked surprisingly.

"I swear," Lily answered as the two giggled over. They spent the next few minutes talking about things of the past as Lily fell asleep.

~

"Why are you still sitting on the chair," Mary inquired without even looking at Ted.

"Becaauuuseee…I need a beer!" he responded.

"I need a glass full of Margarita. Get me that too, when you go out searching for a beer?" Mary said, grinning. Ted laughed too and then bent forward to remove his shoes. He then pushed himself off the chair and lay on the hard wooden floor. The sheet that covered it didn't make it any softer, but he still tried to make himself comfortable.

After a few minutes of uninterrupted silence, Mary spoke, "Do you know there was a thing going on between the two of us? Me and...and Jason."

"How do you think I convinced him?" he replied.

"No way…what did you say to him?"

"I told him this was his chance to try on you, a chance he'd never have again. He was totally head over heels for you," Ted responded, pressing his palms against his eyebrows and then rubbing his eyes. There was a pang of guilt in his voice that was easily noticeable.

"It's not your fault," she tried consoling him.

"I got him here. I should have stayed back with him," he said with a heaviness in his voice as if it was coming from his soul.

"None of us knew that he'd go missing if we left him alone. I know you cared the most for him, and you would have done anything to keep him safe."

"Yet, I left him alone in the woods," he countered.

"Stop blaming yourself…I should have stayed. It was a great opportunity to spend some time together in silence and solace. Just how it is in the books, I read. Or perhaps, Lily could have been too tired, staying back. It could have been any one of us for all possible reasons, but things happen the way they are supposed to happen," Mary was sitting upright with her legs crossed as she augmented her point.

"Hymn….maybe he was right not to come along in the first place," he continued to show his grief.

"Come here," she said in a soft voice. Her eyes had filled with tears, and she knew Ted wasn't feeling much different.

Ted wiped the tears from the corner of his eyes and stood up. He leaned in closer to Mary and gave her a hug. Ted had one leg on the floor while the other was folded on the bed. He was holding her head close to his chest. After a few minutes, he slowly let go as he straightened his folded leg, kissing Mary on the forehead. He had barely walked a few steps away to get down to his floored bed when Mary stopped him in his tracks, "Come, sleep, next to me."

He turned around and gazed over at Mary. The uneasiness and innocence in her eyes didn't allow him to refuse the request. He turned around, walked toward his bed, and picked up the pillow and the blanket, tossing the two on the bed. He then walked over and lay down.

Mary had always appeared to be a tough woman. Someone who didn't seem vulnerable or afraid of anything. At that moment, she was an entirely new person. She was like a little girl who had lost her way, with her eyes pleading for help.

Ted laid down straight with his chest facing the top wall. His hands didn't move much, but his mind thought of all the times he and Jason had spent together. He was engulfed in the past when Mary got in closer and gave him a side hug. At first, he was surprised, but then he placed his hand over Mary's and began to rub it in an attempt to comfort her. He then turned around and squeezed her close to her heart, feeling a similar force being exerted by her. He fondled her hair and her forehead as the two drowned into sleep.

Mike failed to sleep. He pulled out the phone from his pocket and began looking at the pictures of the college. He truly missed Jason and was awake alone. His mind had begun playing tricks on him. He began wondering about the possibilities of Jason's whereabouts. His thoughts were inclined toward all bad that could have happened. To escape his thoughts, he decided to leave the bed and get on his feet. He needed to divert his mind in any way that he could.

He slowly lifted Lily's arm that was resting on him and slipped his way away from her. He made sure Lily didn't get up. He didn't want to disturb her from her sleep, even though it would have helped him to divert his mind. He walked back in forth in the room, looking at everything that was there. The room didn't have much stuff in it, besides two side tables that had no drawers, two lamps that were covered with rust, and a trunk box that was locked.

Eventually, he looked out the window and decided to peak out in the black sky. With his hands crossed, he looked through the window pane and found the trucker talking to somebody. From a distance, he couldn't tell who it was, but he found the meeting extremely odd. Already having negative thoughts in his mind, he feared they might be planning something against them. In order to be sure, he decided to find out.

He softly opened the door, minimizing the sound it created when moved. He opened it enough for him to make his way out. He closed the door in a similar fashion and began walking toward the main door, hoping it wasn't closed. He didn't want to attract any attention, so he had to be very careful.

As he had wished, he found the door open. He needed to move to the left in order to get closer to them. To ensure his presence wasn't noticed, he made his way around the truck that was parked on the left. He stayed low and managed to get closer to the truck. The voices he could faintly hear a few seconds ago had disappeared. He feared the conversation was over and didn't want the trucker to find him eavesdropping as he made his way back into the house.

He was on the driving side of the truck, and he swiftly moved toward the back. As he got to the edge of the truck, he peeked through to see if there was no one standing there. Upon looking, he found no one there, which he kind of found surprising. He then moved from behind the truck from one of its corners to the other. Once he reached the other side, he peaked on the left of it and found it just as vacant. He was surprised to find nobody. It hadn't taken him that long to get outside. Even if the meeting was over, then why didn't he hear the trucker get back inside? It was all too confusing.

From walking low, he now stood on his feet and stared in front of him to find anything moving. As his eyes searched for motion, he felt there was someone behind him. Within a moment, his heartbeat got rigorously high. He quickly turned around and saw the trucker standing in his face with a wide, evil smile.

He turned around again almost instantly to run and found the ugly-looking man standing in his face. It felt like he was living a nightmare. He had only one option to run in the direction opposite to the house. He didn't take a moment to finalize his decision but instantly ran for his life as he had barely run a few yards when a brick hit him on his back. "Noooo....Getaway...." He yelled as he forced himself back onto his feet, continuing to run.

He was running short of breath, and the brick had caused an injury. After running for a few steps, he tripped over a stone and fell flat on the ground. As he turned around, he found the trucker and the ugly man standing over him.

"Don't worry, he'll take you to your friend," the trucker said, using his little finger to clear out something stuck in his teeth.

The ugly man said in a suppressed voice, "Yes, yes, I'll take you there." He then began laughing profusely.

Mike already had his eyes on the stones that lay right next to him. Within a moment, he grabbed a stone and swung his arm toward him to hit him with it. He managed to get him in the stomach, and the trucker instantly lost balance and held his stomach as he landed on his knees. Mike then kicked and tried to hit Gein with the same stone, but Gein had already moved a few steps back.

"Why do you have to make it hard on yourself?" Gein said, swinging the dagger at him. Mike managed to duck and, with no energy left in his feet, began moving away. He didn't know where he was going or how he was to get away. He wasn't prepared for an attack, so he had no plan in place for it.

He turned around to see how close his predators were and, upon turning, noticed the trucker was aiming to throw a stone at him. Somehow, he managed to dodge the strike but tripped over again.

Gein briskly walked to him and pierced the dagger through his leg, stepping on his feet. He pulled the dagger out, and as he was about to make another strike, the trucker's voice stopped him, "No, Gein, this one's mine."

He held the brick over his face and dropped it down

with force. Mike got his hand in the way, which only lowered the pressure yet struck his face with force. He then took the dagger from Gein and put it through his neck. Blood spilled out of his mouth as his body began to freeze after a few jerks.

"I'll take it from here," Gein said as the trucker tossed the dagger on the ground, wiped the dirt and sweat off his face, and turned around to walk back to his house.

CHAPTER 9

SOMEONE IS WATCHING US

"Mike.....Mike?" Lily called out, looking all around. She found the bed empty and quickly got up, leaning over her knees as her legs rested sideways. She covered her face, trying to rub her half-open eyes so that they could completely open. Assuming he was attending to the bathroom, she lay down waiting for him, eventually falling asleep again.

***

"I thought you had slept," Mary said in a low voice.

"I did happen to rest my eyes for a bit," Ted replied.

"Why did you wake up?" she questioned, elevating her chin to the extent that she could see the side of his face. Ted was still staring at the roof.

"I don't know," he said in a defeating voice. After gulping his saliva and clearing his throat, he added, "What about you? Doesn't seem like your eyes have given you a break."

"Nor my mind," she said with a dull laugh.

"Ok, so let's play a game?" Ted seemed a hint more energetic than he was moments ago. He wanted to comfort Mary in any way that he could.

"A game in the middle of the night?"

"Yes… it just questions, and it's called 'Would you rather,'" Ted explained.

"Ok, and how would we rather play it?" she replied with a brief yet mischievous smile.

"I'll start….Would you rather…unmnm…would you rather lose your vision or your hearing?" Ted asked, stretching on a few words, reflecting on his thought process.

"What do you mean? I'd keep both."

"That's how it's played, Mary. Come on, it's just a game," he insisted.

"I'd rather lose my hearing. I definitely need my eyes," she responded.

"Interesting. Your turn."

"Would you rather have x-ray vision or magnified hearing?" she said as her hand had now made its way across his chest.

"Oh, X-ray vision for sure. Oh boy, it's gonna be crazy," he answered with a freakish laugh.

"Why not magnified hearing? I mean, you'd be able to hear people's thoughts."

"Well, you can have that. I'm not missing out on the X-ray vision," he said as the two laughed.

***

Lily extended her arm while having her eyes closed, trying to get in contact with Mike. Unable to find anyone lying next to her, she sat upright again. This time, she was more scared. Pressing her palms against her cheeks, trying to think where he possibly could be, Lily was getting very uncomfortable.

"I'm going to kill him," she uttered, staring around the room.

She crouched, composing her gestures, fighting fear from overpowering her conscience. She knew Mike wasn't attending to the bathroom because if he had, it wouldn't have taken him so long. The room was pitch black, with enough moonlight entering for her to have some sense of her surroundings. She didn't even have the strength to leave the bed, as she feared she'd run into some ghost if she did.

She used her cellphone's flashlight to see if anyone was there or if anything seemed out of the ordinary. Upon finding everything appeared normal, she switched off the flashlight, locked her phone, and kept staring at the door, hoping it would open any moment with Mike walking into the room.

***

"Would you rather kiss me or the trucker?" Ted chuckled.

Mary elevated her head, putting weight on her left shoulder, as her eyes stared into Ted's. She pulled her lips toward his, and as Ted anticipated the kiss, she moved her lips to his ears, whispering, "Would you rather kiss me on the neck or the lips?"

Ted gently brought his lips in contact with her skin. His hands climbed through her hips, to her back, and all the way to her neck, pulling her hair. He pushed her back, and as she lay straight, he turned over, working his lips through her neck. Gradually, he began kissing her chest as his hands fondled her bosoms.

She pulled him by his t-shirt as their lips met, and soon gentle kisses were replaced by wild contact of their tongues. She quickly pulled his shirt as he unbuttoned hers. She was in her night suit, so she wasn't wearing anything inside. He used his thumb to press against her nipples, feeling the shape of her bosom and firming his grip on them.

***

Lily was growing impatient and uneasy. She never had a strong heart, and being in the middle of nowhere and having lost a friend to the jungle, her intuitions weren't giving her any positive insights. She needed to look for Mike, so she decided to leave the room.

She walked a few steps toward the bathroom, and her feet felt weak. She kept looking behind with every step she took forward to ensure no demons followed her. She pushed the bathroom door open and through the light of her cellphone, peeked inside, and found no one there.

***

The two had loved each other long enough, and their emotions demanded more action. Ted slipped his hands inside her pajamas and felt the softening of her skin. His breath had intensified, and so had hers. He pulled his hand out and unbuckled his belt. Just as he grabbed and dragged her pajamas slightly to get them off her body she interrupted.

"Someone's there," Mary said in a soft voice. "Someone's looking inside."

Ted immediately used his knees to balance his weight as he searched for his shirt and wore it.

"Wasn't the door shut?" Mary inquired.

"It has a weak handle, probably got pulled away by the wind," he tried to reason, hoping they'd get back into the grove without him having to leave the room.

"But I'm sure someone was there," Mary seemed unconvinced.

"Alright, I'll check," he got on his feet, and buckling his belt, opened the door and entered the hallway.

He could see someone standing, and he knew who it was.

"Lily, what's up? Everything ok," he asked, concerned.

"Yes, and no," she was relieved to see Ted but was still very concerned about Mike.

"Tell me, what's wrong, and…and where's Mike?" he asked, gripping her shoulders and projecting how her entire body felt. They were shaking, not very intensely, but a movement was there.

"Mike's gone, I don't know where, but he's not in the room, he's not in the bathroom, he's nowhere. Oh my God, I don't know where he is," she said as tears trickled down her eyes.

"Ok, ok, I want you to calm down. Mike's a smart guy, don't worry. Let's look for him, ok?" Ted comforted Lily, and although he didn't like how it sounded, he didn't show it to her. After all, she needed someone to calm her down and not add to her stress.

Lily shook her head as she wiped tears away from her eyes. She failed to dry her eyes but finding Ted had indeed made the search easier.

"Let's look outside. Maybe he's out getting some fresh air," Ted suggested.

She just shook her head in agreement as the two opened the main door. They looked around but found nothing there. It was silent and dark, and the darkness was haunting. Not taking long, they got back inside.

Ted walked toward the stair that was close to the room where Mike and Lily had settled for the night. As he gently placed his right foot on the first stair, he noticed a passage behind it. He immediately took a step back and walked into the passage. Lily stayed close, right behind him. As he got into the passage, he found a door. He looked at Lily as if seeking her permission to go through. Though, Lily's eyes were clueless and scared.

He knew he had to make the decision independently. He softly opened the door that opened to a small staircase leading to a cellar. The two didn't utter a word and walked down the stairs.

The stairs lead into a small hallway that has a metal bar door. Ted pushed the door but was unable to open it. He tried again with greater force but had no success. Just as he loosened his grip in disappointment, he noticed the door slid an inch to the right, indicating the door was to be slid. He slid the door and entered. Barely a few feet away from the door was a dark blue curtain, hiding everything that lay behind it. As he slid the curtain, the two were shaken by the vision as they stood in disbelief.

The room had a number of corpses chained into hooks. The room had a pungent miserable smell, and Ted and Lily had to cover their faces with their hand to be able to breathe. It was a horrific sight. Every corpse hung without a head, and some were cut in half. A few didn't have hands, which seemed to have been butchered, while other corpses were missing a leg or both.

Lily's expressions were telling the story of her fear and shock. It seemed like a butcher's shop, only the meat wasn't of any animals. Trying to avoid any contact, the two pushed their way through the hanging bodies, trying to make their way to the other end of the room.

Just as they crossed the hanging section, they ran into a glass that was transparent. They could see baskets filled with meat and a refrigeration system in place. There were a number of jars lying on a shelf, and from a distance, Ted captured the sight of one of the jars, which terrorized his thoughts. It seemed to have heads of dead people.

He briskly walked to the jar, avoiding stains of blood that covered parts of the white tiled floor. Lily stood next to the glass of the 4-foot wide and 5-foot long room. The jars were large in size and were covered by a blue plastic sheet. As soon as he managed to get rid of the sheet, he took a deep breath and, with trembling fingers, rotated it to see Mike in it. He immediately pulled his hand away as he stared at it in disbelief. Lily peaked from behind, and witnessing Mike's head, she instantly fainted.

Tears streamed down his eyes as he rushed toward Lily. "Lily, Lily, please....Oh god," he rested her body on the glass door as she refused to gain back consciousness. Ted began crying as he wildly rubbed his hair to calm himself but to no success. He walked back toward the shelf with the jars and rotated the other jar finding Jason's head in it. He pulled back as if the jar had electrocuted him.

He crouched on his toes as he buried his head between his lips. Suddenly he realized that they needed to get out. He slapped Lily on the cheek with enough force to get her back to her senses, but she still gave no response. He looked around for water but felt disgusted to touch anything the room had.

He picked her up, placing one hand below her back and the other below her calves. He tried to walk out without touching any of the corpses lying, which was almost impossible. There were so many hung, with so little distance. As he walked past a few, he hit Lily's head in one of the corpses, and as he quickly tried to get her away, Lily's legs pushed the one on the other side. He somehow managed to keep his balance as he took Lily to the metal bar door. He used his feet to slide the door, but the door didn't move an inch.

He began freaking out, not knowing how he was to get out. He put her on the ground, in the same position as he was holding her. He balanced her body in a way that rested its weight on the wall.

He then began pulling the door with full force, but it seemed locked. He tried to squeeze his hands through the bars, searching for anything that could help him unlock the door, but there was nothing he could find.

He quickly pulled out the cell phone from his pocket. His hands did not cooperate, as the phone slipped out of his hands and fell to the ground after landing on his feet. He quickly picked it up and dialed 911. The phone showed no reception, "Fuck. Fuck Fuck. Fuck Fuck. Fuck…." he kept saying as he dropped to his knees and began crying intensely, hitting his forehead with the top side of his fist.

***

Mary had already buttoned back her shirt as she lay on the bed waiting for Ted. He had taken longer than she expected, but she was too lazy to get on her feet and see what had caught him for too long.

She was still in the mood and eagerly sought the heat radiating from Ted's body. It had been over thirty minutes, and she began feeling it odd. She tightened the waistband of her pajamas and grabbed a cigarette from her bag. As she lit the cigarette and took a few puffs, she slid her feet into her slippers and decided to go to the other room. She knew he'd be there. What else could have taken him so long besides Mike's stupid jokes, she thought to herself.

She creaked open the door and made her way into the hallway. *It's dark out here,* she muttered loud enough for only her to hear. She took another puff and began strolling in the hallway to make her way to Lily and Mike's room. As she got to the door, she stuck her ear at the door to hear what her friends were talking about. She heard nothing. It was very silent. Fear began developing inside her. She knocked on the door, and upon hearing no response, she swiftly opened it. The room was empty.

She turned around and looked into the darkness, having no clue what she should be doing next. The cigarette was half done, but she didn't feel like smoking it anymore. She dropped it on the floor and stepped over it.

After giving it some thought, she decided to go upstairs and see if there was something happening there that she was missing out on. As she reached the top stair, she found the trucker sitting on it and enjoying his beer. He kept looking down with a hat covering his face. She knew she hadn't been able to soundproof her movement despite her attempts to walk tiptoed.

As she turned around, the trucker addressed her, "Don't you turn your back on the host." He then lifted his head and began laughing.

Mary tried smiling but couldn't, "Nah, I was just looking for my friend. I'm sorry to have bothered you." She had a strong feeling that something wasn't right;

hence, she did not tell him that she was looking for all three of them.

"No, not at all. There's a beer right next to me. Come on up!"

She didn't think it was the best idea to give him company, and so she refused, taking leave.

The trucker, however, wasn't going to let her return, "Be. My. Guest."

He had said it in a tone that Mary knew she couldn't refuse. She wasn't someone who'd surrender that easily, "I'm not feeling very well. Maybe later."

"Be. My. Guest." This time he said it in a harsher voice, with a fiercer look. She knew she couldn't turn away the offer, no matter how much she hated it. She slowly began climbing the remaining stairs in the trucker's direction.

CHAPTER 10

CANNIBALS!

"There has to be something," Ted mumbled to himself as he quickly got on his feet and headed for the room with the glass door. He had to break out, and with all the saws and breaking knives there, his best shot was cutting the steel bars.

He entered the glass room, and his eye went straight to the jars. He felt grossed out and scared to see human flesh ripped and torn mercilessly, lying around all corners of the cellar.

"You got this," he took a deep breath and began looking for any tool he could get his hands on. He stood facing the steel table. He searched through the bowls filled with blood and organs. He barely looked for a minute and then turned away to puke on the floor. He had his hands on his knees, and after throwing up, he began crying out of helplessness. He cried for a long minute and then immediately wiped off his tears, "Come on, god damn it."

He dropped to his toes to look for some tools in the lower compartment of the steel table when he heard a noise. He knew he had company. He quickly tried to get hold of anything he could get his hands on, and he somehow managed to get hold of a hammer.

He immediately got on his feet and looked for a spot to hide. He heard the sounds of a whistle and flinched his eyes. Fear was filling up inside him, and he began to shiver slightly.

The whistling sound stopped as he heard a heavy voice demanding his attention, "Helloooo, your friend here misses you."

Worried about Lily and not being able to find a decent spot to hide, he decided to use attack as a form of defense. He stormed through the door, attempting to strike the trucker, but the man he saw was far scarier and creepier than the trucker. It was Gein.

Gein passed a smile as Ted stopped in his tracks. There were corpses landing between him and his predator. He yelled and approached Gein, "You son of a bitch." Gein picked up a cup filled with blood and spilled it at Ted as Ted moved a step behind. He hit his back on a corpse and, out of disgust, immediately pulled forward.

"Why do you have to make it difficult for yourself," Gein said in disappointment. He had an axe in his hand.

With shivering hands, Ted ran for Gein again, and Gein dodged him between corpses. He slashed him with a hammer, and Gein ducked as the hammer hit a half-body hooked to the ceiling. Blood spilled out and covered part of his face. The hammer slipped out of his hand as he tried wiping blood from his face. As he bent low to get a grip on the hammer, Gein kicked it away.

Gain whistled again and then started laughing profusely. Ted turned away to make his way to the hammer when he received a blow on his leg. Gein had hit him with the axe. The axe had pierced his flesh, torn his muscles, sticking inside his leg. Facing intense pain within a moment, his loud scream echoed in the cellar. He fell face down, and his body felt numb.

Gein stepped on his calf and, with force, pulled out the axe. Another loud scream escaped his chest. The pain was unbearable. His hand landed close to the hammer, which was at an arm's distance. He picked it up and threw it at Gein with full force. Gein tried to dodge the flying hammer but got hit on the edge of his shoulder.

He lowered his eyebrows, squeezed his eyes, and with a wrinkling nose, tried to control the pain caused by the strike. The next moment, he began laughing loudly, and the laughter was terrorizing. He walked up to him and struck his other leg with the axe. A loud squeak escaped his lips, and Ted lay there unconscious.

"I will kill you. I am a hero. Blah blub blah," Gein said in a sharp made-up voice, imitating Ted. He then laughed as he stepped on his thigh to pull the axe out. Ted had lost a lot of blood.

As Mary reached the topmost stair, the trucker stood up. The way he looked at Mary made her very uncomfortable, which was evident on her face, despite her trying to disguise it behind her smile.

"Don't worry. No one else can harm you," he said with a wide smile. His eyes seemed evil.

"No one else?" Mary wasn't sure if it was a good idea, but she still said it.

"Yes, yes, don't worry. Follow me," the trucker repeated, leaving her concerns unaddressed. Mary wanted to run away at that very moment, but she had to see where her friends were.

The trucker moved a few steps and opened a door,

gesturing her to enter first. Mary slowly walked up to the door, looking at the trucker and the door. She had a strong feeling that this visit wasn't going to end well. She did as was asked.

The trucker didn't move his eyes away from her for even a small instant, and the attention was very unsettling. She entered the room that was filled with antique items. It appeared as a souvenir shop, only if it weren't in a room in the middle of nowhere.

"These are all gifts from my guests," the trucker said as he walked behind him. Mary crossed her hands and clenched her fists tightly. She was prepared for an attack from the man who appeared as a gorse.

The room had a wooden table placed in the center, which was covered with souvenirs and antiques of different sizes. There were lockets, wristbands, and wallet mirrors on one side of the table. In the middle were three phonographs, all varying in size and shape. On the other corner of the table were small decoration pieces made of glass and steel.

Besides the table, the room had two bookshelves that were loaded with books. The dust that covered the shelf showed how the books had been untouched for a long time. The only shelf on the other side of the room had a glass door, which was locked. Inside the shelf were antique guns. The guns were so many that she couldn't even count them.

"Why are you showing me this?" Mary asked, as playing along was becoming extremely difficult for her.

"Why would I?" the trucker stood very close, and even though she wanted to push him away a few yards, she still kept her calm and continued conversing.

"I don't know. Maybe, you want me to add something to your collectibles."

"I don't ask for stuff from people. I get it," the truck said with a wide grin.

Mary didn't know what else she could say, so she turned around and began strolling toward the bookshelf. She just wanted to get away from the man.

Gein tied up Ted's body upside down and hooked him up. His body hung like the many. The difference was his skin was intact, while the rest were already butchered. He tied Lily to a chair, tying her hands behind her back and stuffing cloth in her mouth. He spilled water on her face to get her back to consciousness. Lily opened her eyes, and the sight she woke up was worse than the sight she had lost her consciousness to.

She couldn't breathe, nor could she clear her eyes that were like clouds heavily raining. Gein used a cloth that appeared to have stains of blood to wipe her eyes. She tried pulling her head away, but she was tied, and Gein easily rubbed it on her face.

"It'll get better. Stop crying. I hate women who cry," Gein said, clenching her cheeks so tight that it hurt her.

He took a peeling knife and began peeling his skin. He seemed an expert at it, doing his everyday thing. Lily couldn't take the sight and fainted again.

"You see that picture?" Gein picked up a frame on the table and, rubbing the dust from it, passed it on to her.

Mary shook her head.

"She was the town's mayor."

Mary raised her brows and depicted a fake smile showing her lack of interest.

"Let me tell you her story," the trucker said, sitting at the edge of the table on the only corner that could accommodate him. It was the corner close to the bookshelf.

"Her name was Marianne, and she was fairly popular in the neighborhood."

"Ahan."

"Then one day, she went missing," he leaned forward closer to her face, "just disappeared." He joined his finger and opened them, gesturing for her sudden disappearance.

Despite not wanting to show much interest, she asked out of curiosity, "Disappear where?"

"It is said that a man butchered her and cooked her for dinner," he said, leaning further in as there was barely a foot distance between the two.

She took half a step back as her feet collided with the lowest part of the bookshelf, "and the rest just disappeared?"

"One after another, they were all taken down by this cannibal until no one survived," he moved back.

"And you? How come it did not come for you?" Mary didn't hesitate to advocate her curiosity.

"Guess I was lucky," he said with a straight face.

He spilled a jug of blood on her face, and she woke up

instantly. She moved her head around to get rid of the blood as if it were something placed on her.

"It's ok, sweetheart. It's your friend's blood," Gein said as he continued peeling off Ted's skin. He had already peeled off half his skin, with only his upper body left.

Lily tried to scream and yell, but she couldn't do anything. She began sweating, imagining herself to be next. She pissed in her pants as Gein continued to peel off the skin.

"Don't you look away, DON'T," Gein yelled, grabbing her by the hair and forcing her to look in Ted's direction. Her face was pointing toward Ted's body, but she tightly shut her eyes. Gein used his fingers to open her eyes with force. She, eventually, had to watch him peel off his entire skin.

The trucker picked up a ring lying on the table and grabbed Mary's hand, "Here, this is for you."

Mary tried pulling away but had no success, "let go of me. I'm telling you to let the fuck go," she yelled at the top of her lungs.

"Or, what will you do, you little beauty," the trucker responded, twisting her hand behind her back while covering her chest and gripping her other fist with his other hand.

"You smell so nice," he added as his nose got in contact with her neck.

Mary tried to get distant, but none of her attempts were successful.

"Do as I say, and you live," he said as he felt her body with his. He used his fingers to caress her butt, and Mary stopped to resist. She knew she couldn't break free from him this way. She instead shook her head to show she wasn't going to rebel.

He slowly let go of her hand as he grabbed her butt. Mary made the most of the opportunity and grabbed one of the books. The trucker tried following the motion of her hand to get a grip on it, but before he could, she struck his head with the sharp corner of the book cover with full force. The trucker lost his balance as she got free from his hold and stormed out of the room.

"You nasty little bitch," the trucker screamed as he followed her out of the room. By the time the trucker got to the stairs, she was on the last step. The trucker ran behind her, skipping and jumping through the stairs. Mary opened the main door and ran outside. She ran into the woods and hid behind a tree.

She pulled out the cell phone from her pocket and tried calling one of her friends. The phone showed no reception, "shit," she said in a trembling voice. She heard someone approaching close from the sound of steps landing on rustled leaves.

The trucker kept looking for her in the distance. He knew she couldn't have gone far since he had seen her enter the woods and had run behind her. He moved very slowly, knowing she was somewhere there.

The sound stopped coming, and she felt even more scared. She was panting and crying, with her hands joined in prayer. The trucker's search had failed to locate her, and she remained still in her position. He again began walking, and the sound pierced through her ears. She then heard the sound of a loading gun. He fired in the air, and as soon as the bullet left the barrel, her head jerked as if the bullet had hit her.

From moving forward, the trucker began moving sideways, and after a small stroll, he saw her hair dancing with the wind, visibly from the edge of the tree. The trucker smiled and whispered to himself, "Pity, you're all the same."

The bruise on his head wasn't deep, but it leaked a few drops of blood. He scratched his bruise, and upon noticing blood, he licked it with a smile. He moved a few steps closer to her very slowly but still couldn't avoid the noise. Not wanting to chase her more, he aimed his gun at what was visible. He fired another shot, and it went inches wide from her head. She saw the bullet crash into a tree in front of her.

She instantly knew the trucker had seen her, and she began running again. The trucker looked toward the sky in disappointment and shrugged his shoulders, covering his face with a brief smile. He began following her. This time, he didn't run. After running for a few minutes, she hid behind another tree.

She checked her phone again, hoping the call would connect, but nothing worked. She sat low, hoping he wouldn't see her this time. She had her hands over her knees and her forehead resting on her forearms.

She heard footsteps approaching her, and she froze in her position, hoping to remain unnoticed. Suddenly the trucker appeared in front of her, and she tried getting on her feet to run again, but the trucker immediately shot her.

Lily heard footsteps coming down as she watched Ted's body being butchered. The trucker walked in and threw Mary's body on the floor, saying, "How're we doing here?"

Gein responded, "Almost done. Dinner will be ready in an hour."

The trucker then dragged Mary by the hair and took her to the backside of the cellar away from her sight. He returned to Lily, "You hungry?"

Lily couldn't answer. Fear had made its way into her bloodstream, and she couldn't move. The trucker sat on his knees, and Gein joined.

"It's ok, honey," the trucker said to Lily as he played with her strand of hair, then moved his hand to caress her face. Lily felt disgusted, but she didn't move.

"Yes, we're cannibals, but what so odd about that? Is that odd?" Gein said, looking toward the trucker.

"Not at all. It's the new thing. You'll get used to it," the trucker said, not moving his eyes away from her.

Lily finally tried to yell with full force, but the stuffed piece of cloth suppressed her voice.

"Don't be like that, little bitch. I want you alive," the trucker said, wiping her forehead with his sleeve and then kissing her again.

"Little bitch," Gein repeated and began laughing insanely.

Lily was strapped to the chair for the entire day. The trucker did visit her on a couple of occasions, but she refused to respond. She was offered food that she knew was human meat, and she couldn't even think for a moment about taking a bite from it, despite starving, having not eaten anything for two days.

The next day, she saw Gein enter the cellar and take some meat for cooking. She just looked at him with total surprise, as if he wasn't a human but an alien. By the end of the second day, the trucker unstrapped her. She got off her chair and immediately moved to the corner of the room, where she sat in the corner tightly, holding her legs and looking around out of fear. Her sense of smell was no longer affected by the smell of blood, and she kept staring at the corpses.

The trucker kissed her on the forehead and hugged her as she sat crouched in one corner. She didn't pull away from the trucker, but she still didn't say another word. The trucker tried feeding her with food, but she still didn't open her mouth. The trucker left the dish with food, hoping she'd eat from it later, but when he returned the next day, he found the food untouched.

"If you want to die, Gein can make it easy for you, but do you want to die that way? You deserve to live," the trucker said with a softness in his voice, which made its way into her ears, but reflexes still failed to register what was being told.

She felt weak. Her eyes had dried up, and her clothes were a mess. She seemed like a dumb person who couldn't understand a word that was said to her, and nor could she speak. She just sat there staring at one point. The regular visits of the trucker had not made it any easy, even though the trucker had been polite with her.

After four days, the trucker managed to get water down her throat, but that was it. She still didn't eat. The trucker kissed her on her lips. She didn't move. She had her heart beating and her lungs contracting and expanding, but she was just as dead as the corpses in the room.

Finally, after one whole week, she took the first bite, and within a few minutes, she ate everything that was in the dish. She didn't care whose meat it was or how it tasted. She just ate all of it, expressionless, like an animal.

CHAPTER 11
YOU ARE MINE NOW!

A few months later…

"I need to take a swim," Joe insisted.

"And I need a sauna bath. We all can't get what we want, isn't it?" Alex said in his British accent.

"Well, I don't know about you, but Mother Nature has a lot more for me than it does for you," he winked and began to tie up his shoelaces.

"I wouldn't have minded swimming if it were some sexy ladies accompanying us, and by the way, who suggested an all-boys summer camping?" said Raj. He was short in height and had a dark complexion but an exceptional sense of humor. He always kept the guys laughing.

The camping site had six camps settled around the fire.

Each camp housed one person, and so there were six of them. In the distance, they had parked their dirt bikes, five of them. Since Raj didn't ride, he kept on switching from one ride to another throughout the journey.

The previous night the boys were really tired after long hours of riding and crashed in their camps as soon as they were done setting them up. So, besides the camps and a few logs of burnt wood, there wasn't anything else lying around.

"I'm coming with you. I'm pretty sure if you run into someone by chance, you won't be able to score," Raj commented with a grin.

"Says the person who hasn't been able to find a date the entire semester," Joe responded.

"Well, my standards are high," Raj said, moving his lips sideways as if suppressing his laughter at his own statement.

"Yeah, whatever," Kenneth added as he, too, got on his feet.

Within no time, the entire crew was off the campsite, touring the woods in search of a lake or a river. The boys were fully pumped and energetic. They were laughing and messing around, sipping from beers and puffing on cigarettes. The sound of their laughter could be heard from a distance, but they didn't care any less because, for all they knew, they were alone in the woods, far away from any population.

After a tiring walk through the jungle, they managed to find a promising sight. The pursuit of finding water came to an end as Conner spotted a lake, "Guys, this way, follow me."

"Never thought he'd be a leader," Raj said with a titter. Joe gave him a tired look and shrugged his shoulders.

"You've gone bonkers," Alex said, raising his brows.

"Have I?" Raj replied in a poor attempt to copy his accent.

As the rest followed Conner, they noticed him standing still, closely looking at something. One after another, the boys joined him, and their reactions weren't any different.

The lake looked beautiful, surrounded by trees on all sides. The water appeared to be crystal clear, and the humming of the birds added to the sight's aesthetics. It wasn't the calmness of the water or the serenity of the rustling leaves that had captured their attention. Neither was their attention centered on the sun rays making their way through the trees, reflecting on parts of water, changing its color from blue to an attractive green. What had caught their eyes was the beauty of a young woman who looked exceptionally beautiful in her swimsuit.

Even though the guys had been there for a bit now, she still seemed to have not noticed their presence as she stroked her way through the water.

"Is she real?" Raj said with his eyes frozen on her.

"No, she's a fairy," Brad answered. Although Brad wasn't very talkative, he couldn't resist complimenting her beauty.

Joe placed his backpack on the ground, took off his shirt, and dropped his pants. In his boxers, he was ready to jump into the lake.

"I might not stand a chance; why aren't you scoring?" he said with a giggle as he strived forward to get into the water.

In response, Raj imitated fake laughter, took off his shirt to join him, and so did the rest. The guys didn't jump in close to her to ensure she didn't feel uncomfortable from their presence, even though each one of them was fancying his chances.

Before any of the guys could swim toward her, since she was on the other side of the lake, she swam to the edge and walked out. For the guys, it was a sight to watch. Her swimsuit complimented her figure. Her hips were narrow and round, along with her thick thighs and slender legs. As she stepped out, she bent forward to dry her hair with a towel and then wrapped it around her body. She then sat on the grassy area as if sitting on the beach sunbathing.

"What is she doing here alone?" one of them mumbled.

"Let's find out," Joe replied and began swimming in her direction. By then, she was leaning behind with her weight centered on her elbows. She looked like a model, with her bosoms raised as her head tilted behind, resting on her shoulders. The towel no longer hid her beauty as she had put it aside.

He got out of the lake and went and sat close to her. She opened her eyes for a brief moment, acknowledging his presence, and then shut them again. Joe was moved by her confidence.

"Ahem, ahem," Joe forcefully cleared his throat to demand her attention.

The guys had their attention centered on Joe. He had a decent reputation when it came to girls, so most of them were confident that he'd do well.

"Cut down on the smokes if the coughing persists," she said with a chuckle.

It seemed like a good start. "Hi, I'm Joe," he started to get a conversation going.

"Hello," she gave a brief response.

"Are you here alone?" he inquired.

"No, you're here," she answered.

"I'm here," he repeated with a snicker.

Silence prevailed for a minute when Joe attempted once again to strike up a conversation, "I didn't catch your name."

"Of course, you didn't."

"Alright, I'd…. I'd probably get going," he said, feeling his chances were slim.

She suddenly sat straight and crossed her legs. The swimsuit was very revealing, as her bosoms were bulging out. Joe couldn't resist but look in admiration. She lifted her chin to scratch her collarbone while leaning an inch forward. The posture was very seductive, and Joe couldn't believe his luck. He thought he had made the right decision to speak to her.

"So Joe, what brings you here?" she finally asked a question.

"You," he giggled.

She passed a faint smile, enough to show she didn't mind the joke.

"And you?" he asked in return.

"You," she said with another faint smile.

Joe found the responses a little odd, as they seemed sarcastic and superficial. Regardless, he didn't care much.

"I live down here," she answered.

"Down here? I mean, I didn't see any residential area on our way here. Is there a community or something here?"

"No, it's just my friends and me. I just like it here. It's very calm," she responded.

Joe wondered if her friends were girls. He figured his gang would love to know there were more girls there. Without giving it much thought, he assumed luck was favoring him and ruled out her friends being guys.

"I'm sure my friends would love to meet them," he tried to make a case.

"Same. Mine would be ecstatic."

"Ecstatic, wow," he thought to himself. He thought they lived alone in the woods, and with not many guys around, they wouldn't have the bar too high.

"Then let's plan something," said an excited Joe.

"Hmm, we're living in this cabin in the woods. It's a nice place, small but sufficient. It's two more friends and me. Why don't you join us for dinner?"

"Definitely, but where exactly is it? It isn't easy navigating around here, especially with signals dropping every now and then," he stated.

"Hmm, well, in that case, I'll show the place to you, and then we can tread back and take the rest. What do you say?"

"I mean, can't we all just go together?"

"My friends might get overwhelmed with too many guys coming at once. Let's go meet them first, just so they get comfortable, and then the rest can join," she said in a convincing tone.

Joe couldn't care any less. He wasn't thinking about the guys but weighing his chances of spending some intimate time with this beautiful girl.

"Sure, let me just go over and tell the guys about the plan," he suggested.

"Come on, the guys can wait, just tell them we'll be back in a bit," she said, holding his hand. He could sense that she wanted the same thing as he did, and taking the rest would make it difficult for the two to spend some time alone.

"But my clothes are right there."

"You won't need them," she replied.

"Sure," he got on his feet and yelled from a distance, "Guys, I'll be back in a bit."

"Son of a bitch," Raj exclaimed with excitement in his eyes. The boys joked around for a bit as the two began strolling away.

"You didn't tell your name," Joe asked as they walked for a couple of yards.

"Lily," she said, extending her arm.

"Nice to meet you, Lily," Joe answered, shaking her hand. She locked her eyes on his for a moment as she loosened the grip and began walking.

After a long hour, the guys were tired of swimming, so they settled on the grass, waiting for their friend's return.

"I hope he's safe," said Brad out of concern.

"Oh boy, he'd be having the time of his life," Conner countered.

As the boys were discussing the whereabouts of their friend, Lily grabbed their attention as she came walking from a distance.

She was dressed in denim shorts and tank tops while holding a basket in her hands.

"You boys waiting for your friend?" Lily questioned in a high voice as she got close enough to be heard.

"Yes, why don't we see him?" Raj said, getting up.

"You will soon. You all must be tired here, have some sandwiches," she said, placing the basket on the ground. She opened the basket and removed a box that was stuffed with sandwiches. The boys were hungry, and quickly the food was distributed among them.

"Where's Joe?" Alex asked.

"He's with my friends. I'm here to take you to him. He was supposed to come with me, but well, he preferred staying back," she said with a notorious look, hinting to the guys that he was having a good time.

The guys quickly munched on the sandwiches excitedly.

"What is this? These taste delicious," Conner questioned as he took the last bite from his sandwich.

"I'm glad you liked them," she said with a weird smile. Conner didn't like it, but he didn't say anything.

"Can I have another one?" Brad requested.

"I'm afraid this is the last one you'll have," Lily answered with an intimidating look.

Brad looked at her in surprise, and before he could have her explain her statement, his vision began to blur out.

"What is happening to me?" he said without being able to keep his balance as he slid sideways, lying flat on the ground. Around the same time, his friends began collapsing one after another, and within a few minutes, they were all unconscious. Lily wore a proud smile, and placing the box back into the basket, she placed its cover on it and lifted the basket. Off she went, with a smile on her face.

Alex was the first one to open his eyes, "Bloody hell, mate," he blurted out as he wrestled with the ropes to free himself from its grip. He was tied to a chair in a room that had an unbearable pungent smell.

Next to him was another chair, which Conner was tied on. He was still unconscious.

"Ok, so you're next?" said Gein with a wide, evil smile. He walked up to him, grabbed him by the hair, and pulled his head back as he slit his throat with the knife he was holding in his other hand.

Alex's body jerked multiple times as blood poured out in a stream. Gein washed his fingers with the stream of blood and smelled it.

He then dragged his body, taking it inside the steel bar door. He then returned with a bucket and wiped off the blood that covered the floor. The last one was left, who still hadn't gained consciousness. Gein sat right behind him, waiting for him to open his eyes. He always wanted his victims to see their endings. He enjoyed watching the fear in their eyes.

Mangled bodies lay in one corner, one piled up over another. There were five bodies there, as the sixth was already butchered. Gein was cutting Joe's body into smaller pieces to prepare for dinner.

The trucker stood calmly, sipping from his beer and watching Gein chop the pieces of meat. They both heard the sound of someone stepping down the stairs. Gein looked at the trucker for a brief moment as the trucker passed half a smile. The sound began getting louder as the person had now approached closer.

Next came the sound of the sliding of the metal door. Gein continued doing what he was without turning around to see who was there. The trucker's reaction wasn't any different. With one leg straight and the other partially folded and crossed over the other, he took another sip from his beer.

He was hugged from behind and kissed on the cheek. It was Lily. She looked around and saw the bodies piled one over another as she wrapped her arm around the trucker's waist.

The trucker turned on his right to kiss Lily on the lips. She then said, "Honey! See, I brought dinner."

Gein turned around and looked at the trucker. The two began laughing out loud as Lily's face was covered with a wide grin.

www.ingramcontent.com/pod-product-compliance
Lightning Source LLC
Chambersburg PA
CBHW061343160726
47995CB00001B/158